# A Candlelight Ecstasy Romance ®

## "ELEGANT," HE SAID, WATCHING HER LIGHT THE CANDLES.
## "I FEEL I SHOULD WEAR BLACK TIE."

He ambled closer to her, a flicker in those blue eyes that she couldn't read. His arm snaked around her waist. "I'll have my kiss . . . then I'll change for dinner." Dan's mouth descended slowly. A millimeter from hers, he paused. "Some women set their husbands up for a fall when they wine and dine them in style. Is that what you're doing to me?"

"How could that be?" Val whispered back. "We're not married." She nipped his bottom lip and watched him flinch.

"True." His lips took hungry possession of hers. When he released her, Val touched the corner of her mouth with her tongue, watching his eyes follow the movement. "What a caveman you are tonight."

"You're not so bad yourself." Dan ran his forefinger over his lower lip. "What do you think we're trying to prove . . . to each other?"

# A CANDLELIGHT ECSTASY ROMANCE ®

# LOVERS' KNOT

*Hayton Monteith*

*A CANDLELIGHT ECSTASY ROMANCE* ®

*To my father,*
*who taught me to believe in myself,*
*and to my mother,*
*who was there . . . always there*

To Our Readers:

We have been delighted with your enthusiastic response to Candlelight Ecstasy Romances®, and we thank you for the interest you have shown in this exciting series.

In the upcoming months we will continue to present the distinctive sensuous love stories you have come to expect only from Ecstasy. We look forward to bringing you many more books from your favorite authors and also the very finest work from new authors of contemporary romantic fiction.

As always, we are striving to present the unique, absorbing love stories that you enjoy most—books that are more than ordinary romance.

Your suggestions and comments are always welcome. Please write to us at the address below.

Sincerely,

The Editors
Candlelight Romances
1 Dag Hammarskjold Plaza
New York, New York 10017

# CHAPTER ONE

Val stared at herself in the vanity mirror, eyeliner pencil poised in her hand. The idea had come into her mind like an exploding light as she made up her face. Dan was still asleep in their bedroom. "No. Don't be silly," she murmured to her image. "It's crazy." She stood, her long curvaceous body having only a lacy bra and bikini pants to cover it. She placed the flat of her hand on her abdomen. "I've never wanted children. At thirty-two, I consider myself past the age . . ." She muttered as though she would convince the woman in the reflection.

She looked toward the bedroom as she heard Dan turn in his sleep and mutter. He often talked in his sleep, that big hulk of hers, she smiled to herself. It made her heart pound a little just to think of his looks. His six-foot-four-inch, one-hundred-and-ninety-nine-pound build looked more the physique of a twenty-year-old than a thirty-year-old quarterback for the NFL football team named the New York Titans. He had already been divorced from his high school sweetheart two years when Val had met him at a party given for the Super Bowl contenders last January.

Now six months later, Val had the uneasy feeling that what they had between them couldn't continue. Oh, the passion between them hadn't abated, but deep differences about the direction their lives should go in kept erupting with disquieting frequency.

Dan fully intended to fulfill his contract and quarterback another year, even though his separated shoulder gave him trouble and his knee was becoming a problem. They had many arguments about it.

Val would soon be fully committed to the job of anchor woman she had almost decided to accept with a talk show on CBC in San Francisco. Her argument that Dan had more than enough money, with his chain of hotels not only in North America but also in Bermuda, the Bahamas, and Jamaica, was met with his argument that she should be content to keep the lesser job in New York of cohost on the morning show with Bud Dailey.

For the past few weeks the coolness between them had been building, the separations caused by the television commercials and promotional pieces that were filmed in Florida having a wedging effect on the relationship.

She stared into the mirror, reseating herself. "Why would you ever think of getting pregnant now? Now . . . when you can feel the gap between you and Dan widening?" Val grated to her image.

She put her head in her hands. "Forget it. It's a stupid idea."

Unbidden, she recalled how she had first met Danilo Cravick, hard-bitten football player of English, Slavic, and Greek background who had come out of the coal fields of Pennsylvania to take Notre Dame by storm then rise into the NFC as the outstanding quarterback of the league. Danilo, who had worked as a dishwasher and cook when he wasn't working out on the field. Danilo, who had taken a few hundred dollars and with his two uncles had begun the chain of hotels called Wrens, after the bird that his English-born mother had described to him as being on her family emblem. Danilo, of the tall, black good looks, a dark handsomeness relieved only by the blue eyes that had come to him from his mother. He looked all Slav and Greek as his father's family were. His hair was the midnight black of the anthracite coal of his home region, his skin had a light swarthiness to it that would never burn

10

in the sun. Arrows of black hair covered his chest, dark hair on his arms and legs.

"What a contrast we are!" Val grimaced at her reflection, her golden eyes and almost platinum hair accompanied by a pinky-cream complexion. Though she was considered taller than average at five feet eight inches, her willowy, lissome figure and long legs further enhanced the look. Her finishing school walk—chin up, tummy tucked —had an elegant, inbred grace.

"Valentina Gilmartin, no wonder your father disapproves of your relationship with Dan. He is not what you were taught to think of as a man at Villeneuve Finishing School in Switzerland." She grinned as she thought of the pink-icing life she'd led even after her marriage to Craig Gilmartin. "If Craig hadn't died in that airplane accident, we no doubt would have bored one another to death." She had a shadowy vision of the man who had made her a widow at twenty-three when the plane carrying him and other gambling friends had crashed en route to Atlantic City. They had been married two years, and though they were brought up in similar fashion, had been schooled much the same, had many mutual friends for years, they had little in common except tolerance of each other's foibles.

Val sighed and slipped on a dressing gown to go downstairs to the kitchen of their brownstone in the West Sixties of Manhattan. No, I certainly didn't have much of a marriage to Craig, she thought. She poured herself a cup of coffee from the percolator sitting on the sideboard in the morning room.

Val picked up the paper from its place on the sideboard and sat down at the table, appreciating the sun streaking the tablecloth with warmth. She tried to read, to blot out the tumultuous thoughts from her mind.

After minutes of reading and rereading the same sentence, she slapped the paper down on the table and leaned

11

back in her chair, sipping her coffee and letting thoughts of Dan mushroom in her mind.

It didn't seem seven months ago that they had met and six months since they had begun living together. It seemed a lifetime. Sometimes it shredded her insides to realize that life had seemed to take on luster, glory, and joy when Dan Cravick had come into it.

Memory catapulted her back to that slushy, cold night in January when she and Binkie Lawler were returning from the ballet and he convinced her that as part owner of the Titans he should stop by the hotel where an interview and reception were being held to honor the team. The men would be leaving the next day for final training in California before fighting it out in the Super Bowl at Pasadena the following Sunday.

The Rolls Royce pulled up in front of the Waldorf-Astoria with a swish of wet wheels.

"How ever did you get those prehistoric creatures into the Waldorf, Binkie? You must have signed a huge damage clause." Val had laughed at her childhood friend, who, though much richer than she had been and certainly more indulged, still managed to be an astute businessman, with the Titans being both a plaything and a tax write-off.

Binkie grinned at her. "The house at Malibu is collateral . . . but I assure you my team will never tear up the old place. They may be big, but they are gentlemen." He looked down his rather sharp, thin nose, his balding blond head glistening in the lights of the hotel. "My dear, you may laugh . . . but you may also be surprised to hear that one of those persons you so freely describe as a near-Neanderthal has a law degree, has passed the bar in New York, and is a partner in the Wrens hotel chain."

The Rolls Royce cruised to the opulent entrance to the Waldorf. The chauffeur got out and stood at the open door of the car.

Val had shrugged before alighting from the car, arranging the fox jacket closer to her body in the bite of wind.

She and Binkie had enjoyed the ballet, and she was in a relaxed mood. Since she was going to interview the owners of the football teams competing in the Super Bowl, she let Binkie talk her into coming to the reception honoring the two winners of the AFC and NFC. "I still can't admire men who go out on Saturday or Sunday afternoon and pummel each other like rutting rams fighting over a mate . . . and all this for the loyal support of glassy-eyed television addicts with beer bellies." Val finished out of breath.

Binkie Lawler, born Birtram Kenneth Lawler, took her arm, leading her down the wide lobby to a long hall that in turn led to a small ballroom from which sounds of partying were issuing. "Ummmm, you are a snob . . . about sports. I would never have thought it of you, Val . . . swimmer, tennis and golf devotee that you once were."

"Twaddle, Binkie, dear. Don't try that Yalie pursed-lip stuff on me." Val pinched his hand just before he nodded to the attendant to open the double doors leading to the gathering.

Binkie lifted Val's fur from her shoulders and handed both coats to the cloakroom personnel.

Val fought the rush of blood to her face when she heard a whistle and a laughing comment. She wasn't about to give those pachyderms any ammunition for their mouths by letting her feelings show.

"I'll be right back, Binkie. I just want to freshen up a bit." Val was glad to get to the powder room. Her makeup was still fresh, and her long, form-fitting strapless satin dress was uncreased. The pale caramel coloring made her gold eyes more vivid. For a fleeting second she wished that she had told Binkie that she wanted to wear her fur. Often the larger rooms in a hotel were cool.

Val shrugged and applied the peachy-gold lip gloss to her mouth, tightened the back of dangling topaz earrings, picked up the gold clutch bag, and left the sanctuary of the rest room.

She paused a moment in the short hall just outside the

ballroom, scanning the group of men there and the scattered number of women. None were dressed as formally as she and Binkie. "So?" she muttered to herself. It struck her that she had never been in a room filled with such large men in her life. Not only were they wide, they were tall. Some had teeth missing, some had marks on their faces. Some of them were good-looking. All of them looked hearty enough to wrestle a Kodiak bear.

Val took a deep breath and stepped into the larger room, her eyes in search of Binkie. She saw him across the room talking to a tall, black-haired man who dwarfed him.

Head high, Val glided forward, keeping her eyes on Binkie.

"Ma'am . . . howdy . . ."

A man with shoulders like barn doors stepped in front of her, blocking out the room, almost blotting out the light. There was an elfish charm to his expression and boyish smile. "Would you mind if I told you that I never saw nothin' prettier 'n you even at brandin' time?"

Val's trepidation left her as she felt her own face relax in greeting. "Not if you don't mind me saying that I have never seen anything larger than you in my life."

"Even my mother says that." His grin widened. He looked taken aback when Val put out her hand, then he took it in one of his giant paws, holding it gently. "I'm Bear Dulane from Texas, and I'm a fullback for the Titans. . . ."

"How . . ." Val began when she felt her hand taken from Bear's and held more firmly by another. She blinked at the dark man who had just been talking to Binkie at the bar.

"I'm Danilo Cravick. Everyone calls me Dan." He kept hold of her hand with ease even as he turned to look at Bear. "Get a beer, Bear."

"Dammit, Dan, I saw her first." Bear glared at the other man, then shrugged and was about to amble away.

"Wait . . . ah, Bear, I'll go with you. I'd like a beer." Val had not acknowledged Dan Cravick's introduction.

14

Now she looked at him. "Release me . . . please." Her hand was free, but as she turned to walk with Bear toward the bar, Dan Cravick was on the other side of her.

As Bear handed her a beer, she was aware of Cravick's stare, but she didn't turn her head. When Binkie came up to her, she was relieved to see him.

"Oh, I see you met Dan, Val." Binkie smiled, then looked openmouthed at Bear when he leaned toward him, the gremlin expression replaced by one of bulldog ferocity.

"Is she your girl?" Bear quizzed Binkie.

"Ah . . . well . . . you . . . see I propose to her periodically and she keeps turning me down." Binkie rolled his eyes at Val.

"I keep telling him that I don't believe in marriage." Val smiled at Bear.

"That's what she tells me." Binkie accepted a beer from the attendant, looked pained, but sipped it anyway.

"I don't believe in marriage either." Somehow Dan Cravick had turned his body, shielding her from the other two. He lifted his glass and toasted her. "We have something in common." He grinned down at her, and Val felt her stomach tighten.

They talked of many things. She told him that she was interviewing the two owners of the football team before they flew out to California with the team to play in the Super Bowl. He had asked her to come. She had said no.

When he sent her tickets later in the week, she flew out with Binkie, staying in his house at Malibu, then driving to Pasadena.

She watched Dan that day, amazed, alarmed, excited at his talent and speed. When he threw one down the middle and then was buried under a ton of flesh Binkie called defensive linemen, she cringed.

"Stop that," Val shouted. "Don't do that to him, you . . . you monsters!" She felt such a surge of anger she wanted to rush out onto the field and pummel the defense.

15

"For God's sake, Val," Binkie had hissed, clutching her arm. "Sit down. Yell, if you must, but not like that."

Val had not sat down. In fact, she had shouted more that day than she had ever remembered doing. Binkie had vowed not to bring her again. He glared at her. "No one threatens to call the police at a game."

When Dan ran off the field the winning quarterback, both fans and teammates trying to lift him to their shoulders, he had come right to where Val was sitting. His head was thrown back, his smile was wide. "For you, baby." He held up the game ball.

Val's heart had pounded for joy, her hands clenched on her arms as though to keep her body from hurtling down the steps of the grandstand and jumping into his arms.

She had seen him after the game in the company of well-wishers and teammates. They didn't get to say much, but Dan was beside her, holding her hand, her arm, his mouth going down to her cheek or her hair on more than one occasion.

"I want to be alone with you," he had whispered.

"Me too." Val felt inarticulate. She, the woman known for the fast patter, quick repartee, was reduced to gulping words and phrases.

They saw each other every waking moment for a week after their return to New York. At the end of the second week, Val was dazed. She wasn't falling behind with her work, but the same heart and soul dedication she had always brought to it was missing. Dan was lifelike and in full color at the front of her mind. When she read her mail in the morning, it was his smile she saw. When she brushed her teeth on rising, she didn't see her gold eyes in the mirror. She saw vivid blue with a dark ring around the iris.

One night they came home from dinner in a little French restaurant, and Dan drove right to his apartment . . . the new one that he had told her he had purchased.

"I bought the building, with my uncles, intending to tear it down, and we decided to renovate instead."

When Val walked in, she was enchanted with the terrace, the window wall, the carpeting in cream to match the walls, the accent colors blue and brown. "It's lovely." She turned to smile at the dark-haired giant who had become such a part of her life.

"Do you like it better than your brownstone?" Dan's face was expressionless, the planes of his rugged features delineated by the fire in the fireplace.

Val had not expected the question. "Well . . . I like them both . . . but . . . I think I still prefer my brownstone."

"Good. I'll move in with you." He walked toward her, the set expression in his face much like the one when he called signals in the Super Bowl. "Either way, this is the last night we live apart . . . or we don't see each other again." He took a deep breath. "I've been patient with you, Val. I didn't want to rush you . . . because I could sense that whatever experience you'd had with men, you were wary, but I'm going out of my mind." He stopped in front of her. "I don't want to lose you . . . but I have to love you, baby, live with you, come home to you. . . ."

Val turned her back on him, wanting to laugh out loud. "I'm certainly glad you mentioned it. I was going to say something about it myself tonight." She whirled around to face him, chuckling at his surprised expression. "In fact on my lunch hour today I saw just the bed for us. Shall we look at it together?"

"Buy it," Dan croaked, then swung her up into his arms, his mouth taking charge of hers at once. That had been the first night they had made love.

Val blinked her eyes as she sat at the table, glancing dazedly at the paper in front of her. With no effort she could recall the heat of their love that night, how, in a matter of moments, the passion built and seared them so that she had felt almost choked by the depth of feeling that

17

rose in her when Dan had carried her to the bedroom and peeled the clothes from her body with tender loving strokes, murmuring love words to her the whole time.

She had not expected the torching reaction of her body as she clutched his shoulders and gasped with delight.

After that, until Dan was able to move his things to her brownstone, they slept in either one of the places each night. Neither wanted to be separated from the other.

When Mrs. Hernandes poked her head from the kitchen, holding the edge of the swinging doors, and asked if Val would like eggs, she shook her head. Mrs. Hernandes nodded, smiled, and disappeared behind the swinging doors to emerge seconds later with a jug of fresh orange juice.

"You should drink this even though you don't eat as you should." Mrs. Hernandes didn't approve of Val's light meals. Conversely, she was thrilled at the three huge meals a day that Dan could consume.

"Thank you, Mrs. Hernandes. I'll drink this . . . you can be sure." Val thanked her, took the assortment of vitamin pills that Mrs. H. had put out for her, then sat back in her seat and sighed. It was crazy to think of having a child. What did she need with a child? Dan's child? Dark, strong, laughing . . . hers.

The idea went round and round in her head as she went back up the stairs to dress. In a flash of insight she knew she would cherish the child.

Dan was still in bed, so she tiptoed up to the bedside table to pick up her watch and notebook that she usually left there.

"Gotcha." He whirled around from his stomach to a sitting position in bed, pulling her across his knees. "Ummm, I taste orange juice," he said after a deep good morning kiss. "Did you save me any?" He smiled down at her, his one hand running down her cheek to the opening in her dressing gown.

"You know Mrs. H. will make you a gallon of the stuff

18

anyway." Val smiled at him, trying not to let him see how he was affecting her. It angered her to see that clinically assessing look he was giving her as he began to caress her. He enjoyed watching the effect his loving had on her, and it irked her to know that even fully aware of the powerful effect she had on him, he could always mask his feelings better than she.

"Did I ever tell you that kissing your breasts is one of my favorite activities in the world?" He suited words to action, freeing her breasts from the dressing gown and leaning down to take the nipple into his mouth.

"Dan . . ." Val groaned, taking his head into her hands, the feel of his face under her hands its own special erotic stimulus. "You shaved."

"Un-huh. I woke and you weren't here . . . and I wanted to make love to you . . . so I shaved while I waited for my girl to come back to bed."

"I'm not a girl." She squeaked, her voice tremolo from excitement. "I'm two years older than you."

"Bagatelle. We both know that really you're many years younger than I am." He lifted his head. "In some ways . . . you're just a baby."

The idea that had been born that morning surfaced in her mind again. "Babies. You don't like babies. Do you?" She watched him through the curtain of her golden lashes that were naturally black-tipped.

"Babies? How the hell did that come up when all I want to do is think of you?" He nuzzled her neck before lifting her and sliding her down onto the bed next to him.

"Do you like babies?" Val persisted, her fingers twisting the curling black hair on his chest.

Dan looked down at her, his eyes still slumbrous from their touching each other. "Some of the guys tell me that their kids can really get in the way of the loving. . . . As you can see I wouldn't like that." His mouth slid down her body, reheating the part of her that had turned cold.

Val reacted to him as always, her arms going around

19

him in an almost frenzied way as though somehow she could push away time, shut out the world, close them in their own special haven.

The kernel of pain stayed buried deep inside her, the awareness that their parting was a real possibility, but even more, Val knew that she wanted something of Dan, something she could keep and cherish that was part of him.

That day she made an appointment with her gynecologist to talk things over with her. Myrna Deitz was a good obstetrician as well.

"There's no reason that you could not conceive and carry a healthy child full term. The chances of having problems with a pregnancy are greater after thirty we've found, but you are a very healthy woman, Val. Are you thinking of starting a family?" Myrna looked at her over her half glasses.

"Yes." At that moment Val decided.

"Well, since you always know when you ovulate and you are pretty regular, I may be seeing you in a few months."

Val left Myrna's office feeling high. She shopped while she was out and bought lobsters. When she went back to the office, she called Mrs. Hernandes and asked her to fix a salad and a cheese board.

She couldn't get in touch with Dan. He was having some kind of meeting with the owners of the team that day.

Dinner that night was special, and because things had fallen into place at the studio, she was able to get away early and help Mrs. H. with the dinner preparation.

She had dressed in a soft apricot wool dress that had the consistency of silk and swayed about her knees when she walked.

Dan walked into the dining room when she was lighting the candles, his jacket slung over his shoulder, his eyes narrowed on her. "Elegant." The satirical smile lifted one corner of his mouth.

"Thank you." As always when she looked at him, Val had the sensation of running uphill.

"I feel I should wear black tie." He ambled closer to her, a flicker deep in those blue eyes that she couldn't read. His arm snaked around her waist. "I'll have my kiss . . . then I change." His mouth descended to hers slowly. A millimeter from her mouth, he paused. "Some women set their husbands up for a fall when they wine them and dine them in style. Is that what you're doing to me?"

"How could that be?" Val whispered back. "We're not married." She nipped his bottom lip with her teeth, watching him flinch.

"True." His lips hit hers like a ram, his tongue invading her mouth at once, stroking her tongue and teeth, possessing her as he always did.

When he released her, Val touched the corner of her mouth with her tongue, watching his eyes follow the movement. "I taste blood," Val said mildly, her fingernail probing his cheek. "What a caveman you are tonight!"

"You're not too bad yourself." Dan ran his forefinger over his lower lip. "What do you think we're trying to prove . . . to one another?"

Val had a feather of cold on her skin as she saw again that blue marble look deep in his eyes. "Are we doing that?"

Dan kissed her hand, then swung around and walked out of the room. "Be right down." His voice carried back to her as he mounted the stairs.

Val stood there, her hands flexing as she pressed them against the silky wool of her dress. For a moment she wanted to scream and rail against the Fates that had engineered that first meeting with Dan. Wouldn't she have been better off never to have met a man who could tear her apart to bite-sized pieces? "No . . . no." She walked toward the kitchen. Is it better to be stung to death rather

21

than never feeling at all? She berated herself silently. What a philosopher you are Valentina Rogers Gilmartin!

She held open the swinging door that opened to the butler's pantry then walked through to the kitchen. "Mrs. Hernandes . . . you can go now. Thank you."

Mrs. H.'s eyes widened. "I usually stay until eight o'clock, Mrs. Gilmartin . . . but . . . if you don't need me, I really would like to leave early."

"Fine. Everything looks lovely."

"Does the mister know he is having his favorite . . . lobster?" Mrs. Hernandes beamed. Dan was a favorite of hers.

"It's a surprise." Val smiled, feeling her own stomach turn over at the thought of food. Whenever she was upset, even as a child, the one thing she could not do was eat.

She was waiting for Dan in the lounge when he came back downstairs, a vodka martini in her hand.

"Planning on sleeping through the meal?" Dan loped into the room, took the glass from her hand, swallowed some, then grimaced at her. "Tummy upset?"

"A little." Her lips shifted into a smile that had a wobble to it.

He had not returned the glass to her. Now he upended the rest, set the glass on the table, and reached for her. "Stop it . . . right now. I can feel you tensing up, Val. Building walls between us. Stop it."

Val let the air whoosh from her lungs as she turned her cheek against his chest and relaxed. "May I stay like this for the evening?"

"You can stay like that for life, babe. You know that."

Val arched her neck to study his face. A river of words ran through her, but she spoke not one. Was it moments or hours that they held each other and looked into one another's eyes? "Lobster tonight," Val finally whispered.

Dan lifted his head toward the kitchen. "Is that what I smell? I wasn't paying enough attention, I guess."

22

She pulled back from him to take him by the hand and lead him to the dining room.

The candles had burned down a bit by the time they had served themselves and brought the plates to the table.

As was their custom, they sat at right angles to one another so that they could be close and yet look at each other with ease.

"I have to get back to Tampa on Thursday, and I'll be there for a week, babe." He watched her for a moment, then put down his fork and took her hand. "I don't like it any more than you do. Why not come with me?"

She tried to smile at him, but her face felt rubbery. "You've told me so many times that the women hardly see their husbands anyway and that they end up shopping or visiting with each other." She put her hand over his. "At least I have a job to keep me occupied."

"I'd be glad to keep you occupied, lady mine." Dan leered at her, then bent down to kiss the cord of her neck. "Quit the damn job and stay with me."

"I think we've had this discussion before. If you quit football, you could have your office anywhere I happen to get a job." Val bit her lip, wishing she had said nothing as she watched those blue eyes turn to ice.

"San Francisco, you mean." Dan chewed the words then spat them.

"There . . . or any other city." Val felt him withdraw from her.

"My job is as important to me as yours is to you." Dan looked at her.

"I know that," Val began.

"No, Val, you don't. To you football is a barbarian's game played by what you term cretins—"

"I never said that after the first evening." Val gasped, hurt and fear snowballing in her.

"No . . . but your thoughts on football are pretty transparent—"

"Wrong," Val interrupted, jumping to her feet and

23

making her chair wobble. "I don't like football. I never pretended that I did, but it's mostly . . . mostly"—Val was gulping air as she felt tears clog her throat—"because I was afraid to see you hurt."

Dan jumped from his chair, not even turning when it tumbled backwards with a bang. He was around the table and lifting her into his arms cradling her to his expansive chest. "Baby . . . baby, don't cry."

"I . . . I never cry." Val sniffed, willing her eyes to dry.

"I know that. . . ." Dan crooned to her, taking the fine damask napkin at his place and dabbing at her eyes. "You're my sweetheart and I know that you don't want to see me get hurt . . . but, lamb, believe it when I tell you that I don't usually get hurt."

"A separated shoulder is getting hurt. . . ." She lashed at him, her arms holding him around the waist. "A twisted knee that requires therapy is getting hurt." She burrowed into his chest, a shuddering sigh going through her.

For long minutes they stood there, Dan murmuring into her hair, his one hand going up and down her back in gentle massage.

They cleared the table together as they always did, scraping the dishes and putting them in the dishwasher. There were no pans because Mrs. Hernandes always took care of that before she left.

They meandered back to the lounge, arms around one another's waist to sit side by side on the U-shaped couch in front of the fire, listening to Beethoven and sipping cognac that Val privately thought too hot.

Dan took her snifter from her hand after a while and finished the contents. "If I wait for you to drink this, you'll fall asleep. I don't want you asleep when we go upstairs, lady mine."

"I feel wide awake." Val reached up and pulled his head down to hers, her tongue thrusting into his mouth and getting instant response.

Dan's body moved in an almost instantaneous answer,

curving over hers as they fell back on the couch and divested each other of clothing with practiced speed.

It overwhelmed Val to feel such a surge of sensual need. It was always new, always fresh with them. It was always the first time . . . only better . . . always better.

Val groaned as she projected ahead for a flash and saw empty years without Dan; then her being emptied of everything but Dan and the flame between them.

When she felt him swing her high into his arms and stride toward the stairs, she nipped his cheek with her teeth. "I didn't want to go to bed."

"No?" he rasped, taking the stairs two at a time, having no difficulty carrying her.

"No." She purred. "I wanted to seduce you on the Kerman rug in front of the fire."

Dan shouted with laughter as he shoved open the door to their bedroom with his shoulder. "How many times have we made love on that round carpet, do you think?"

"Fifty maybe." Val pulled him down with her onto the bed, she clad now only in panties. "We'll have to go down and get our clothes." She ran a fingernail down his nose. "We don't want Mrs. Hernandes picking up our things and picturing our activities."

Dan tugged the panties from her body, his hands a dark, big-boned contrast to her creamy-complexioned, delicately boned frame. "Angel, Mrs. H. has five children. She doesn't think they came by hot-air balloon." His mouth slid down her skin, making her body writhe with delight.

Val turned to him, her arms tightening around his neck, her face buried against him as she strove to get even closer to him.

"Val . . . Val baby, there's no one like you." Dan folded her closer to him.

25

## CHAPTER TWO

When Dan called Val later in the week to say that he had to be in Tampa much longer than he'd first expected, somehow their rational discussion escalated into a full-blown argument. Val knew that Dan was only doing his job, and though she later realized that she might have been a bit unreasonable, she was too hurt and angry to call back and apologize. She sat up late that night reading with the phone close at hand on the nightstand. Though she had hoped that Dan would call her back, he never did.

In the meantime CBC and their affiliate station Channel 3 in San Francisco began to pressure Val to come out and look over the programing that they were planning. She put them off, wanting to wait until Dan came home and they could talk about it face-to-face.

Binkie flew into town and called her. "Val, since Dan is out of town, have dinner with me at the Colony. I have a surprise for you."

Val sat at her desk making notes for the next day's program in her pocket calendar. "No way. The last time you said that, we had dinner with that fool from Arizona who brought his pet cobra with him and emptied Elaine's on the spot. You were told never to come back, as I recall."

"Wrong on two counts, child. One, the snake was a harmless king snake that became upset when left alone, so David brought him along so he wouldn't get lonely. Two, I am already back in the good graces of the Elaine estab-

26

lishment." Binkie's voice sank from its lofty level to normal. "Besides, by the sound of you, you could use a night on the town. See you at eight. Take a cab. I'll get you home."

The phone crashed in her ear, making Val wince and glare at the offending instrument.

"For two pins I'd let him swing at the Colony," Val gritted to herself, then pictured the long evening she had ahead of her until Dan called her at eleven.

She left the studio at noon, deciding to take a swim at the nearby club rather than eat. The forty laps she set herself whittled off the rough edges she had been fighting all that morning. When she dressed and made up her face, she felt more than equal to facing the task of interviewing a man who had been arrested for rappelling down the side of a high-rise office building in Manhattan.

She was passing a newsstand when a face caught her eye. She stopped and stared at the *Tattler*, a rag she had never purchased, but then it had never had Dan's picture on the front page with a buxom blonde and long-legged brunette dangling from his arms, his hands holding his helmet in front of him. His hair was lank and limp on his forehead, perspiration pasting it there; his eyes had a lazy go-to-hell smile that they often had after a tough game She couldn't stop staring at the picture. It was as though it was Dan himself looking back at her.

"How many times has he told you about these setup pictures?" she muttered to herself, her hand going out to pick up the tabloid as though it had a will of its own

"You say some'n, lady?"

Val looked up at the skinny attendant, his face needing a shave, a cigar in one corner of his mouth, unlit but chewed.

He noticed Val looking at him and took the cigar from his mouth, one end of it quite damp. "Trying to quit. My old lady says I won't get cancer then." He shrugged and put the wet cigar back into his mouth. "You taking that magazine you're squeezin' in your fist there?" He spoke around the cigar.

"What?" Val looked down at her hand that had clenched around the paper. "Ah . . . yes . . . I think so." She fumbled into her shoulder bag for the money.

"That there's Dan Cravick on the front. You're probably like my wife and don't know nothing about football . . . but he's the greatest."

Val smiled at the man and handed him a five-dollar bill. "Yes, he is, isn't he?"

" 'Course he sure does love the ladies . . . so I hear." He handed her back her change and looked suprised when she glowered at him and stalked away.

Back at the studio she tried to uncrease the paper on her desk by smoothing it with her hands.

"He has explained to you many times about the groupies that hang around, about the girls who just want their picture taken with a celebrity of any kind. . . ." Val talked to herself, nodding her head at the same time. "They're damn pretty, just the same." She put her head in her hands. "It's me. I feel guilty about trying to get pregnant and not talking it over with him." She lifted her head and thought about the talk she had had with Myrna about taking special vitamins or something that would help her to get pregnant.

"These things take time, Val. You don't just snap your fingers," the doctor had said.

Now Val shuffled some papers on her desk, rolled the tabloid and put it in her purse, and pressed the button to tell her assistant to send in Butch Delwar, the man who rappelled down the Steward Building.

The afternoon went by too fast. She became caught up in her mail. David Curtis, Program Director, called with an idea that his wife, of all people, had put forth.

"Lisa feels that a program on international gardening would appeal to the female sector of your audience."

"Does she indeed?" Val held her head in one hand and

28

doodled on her pad with the other. When she cradled the phone, she stared at the paper in front of her. She had drawn hangman's nooses across the pad with the name Lisa printed under each one. "What would a psychiatrist say about you, Valentina Gilmartin?" She crumpled up the doodles and tossed them in the basket and looked at the clock, groaning. Seven o'clock! She wouldn't have time to go home first. She called Mrs. Hernandes and told her that she was going out for dinner and wouldn't be coming home to change.

Then she pawed through the selection of dress clothes she kept in the small closet in her office. She kept the clothes there because sometimes she had to go to a function at the last moment that required dressier garments than she wore to work.

She pulled a black satin suit from the closet and held it up in front of her, then nodded. With the ecru silk blouse with the frilly jabot she would be fine for the Colony. She opened a box of shoes, the black peau de soie slings nestled in tissue paper next to a black satin clutch bag. The ring and earrings she would use were in the locked drawer of her desk, a pinkie diamond ring given her by Dan with matching pierced teardrop earrings, also diamonds.

By the time she washed in the ladies' room and applied fresh makeup, then donned the very sheer black nylons that the suit demanded, it was close to eight. She called a cab to take her to the Colony, then took the elevator to the lobby to wait for it.

"Your cab is here, Mrs. Gilmartin." The night attendant approached her as she sat reading the evening paper, her half glasses perched on her nose.

"Thank you, Bill." Val steeled herself automatically to taxi rides, never able to understand how they got from point A to point B without collision.

When she arrived, she overtipped as usual and walked through the door held by the doorman who inclined his head and smiled at her.

When the maitre d' came forward, she smiled. "Mr. Lawler's party, please."

The maitre d' bowed her across the room to a round table set near the wall bounded by potted plants to give an illusion of privacy. With Binkie at the table was another man, tall, aesthetic-looking, rather like Abraham Lincoln with a mustache but no beard. His brown hair was short but had a windswept look that made Val smile. He rose along with Binkie as she approached.

"Hello, Val." Binkie kissed her cheek, then held her chair, waving the maitre d' away. "This is John Dewey. He's with CBC out in San Francisco. John, this is Valentina Gilmartin."

"I would know you without the introduction; I've seen your show," he said.

Val watched him, her hand still in his. "Out in San Francisco?" Her voice was bland.

"No . . . you don't come out to us. When I've been in New York . . . and I didn't have to rush to a meeting, I've turned you on . . . to pass the time." His eyes glinted in laughter.

Val chuckled, realizing that he had known she was skeptical of him.

"Now, tell me why you were smiling when you looked up at my hair. Messy, is it?" John quizzed her.

"No, I was just thinking that your casual windswept look probably took your barber hours to accomplish." Val grinned when he grimaced.

"Damn. I was promised that it would look just as though I'd run my fingers through it."

The three of them laughed.

Val sat back with a very small glass of white wine and felt relaxed for the first time in days.

Dinner was lemon sole, a favorite of Val's. She passed on the wine the men had ordered to accompany the meal and switched to seltzer and lemon.

"So . . . you have been approached by Dean Carver to

30

do the show with him in the morning slot." John Dewey let his hand hover over the cheese board, finally spearing a wedge of fresh pineapple and Brie for his plate. "Is there anything that I can say to convince you to come west, Val?"

Val shook her head, frowning at Binkie who looked back at her, a smile on his face. "I just need time to think things over . . . and then make up my mind."

"Bink tells me that your father lives in California." John nodded to the waiter as he showed them the liqueur.

"Yes. I have a sister and a brother as well out there, but I consider New York my home." Val smiled at the man, fully aware of how attractive he was and just as sure that his charm was wasted on her.

"I have been trying to get Val to come home for years, but she likes the avant-garde existence she leads here." Binkie popped a grape into his mouth, then saluted Val with his tiny liqueur glass. "Try the melon brandy, Val. Good."

"No, thank you." She turned to John. "You must understand that Binkie feels that anyone who works for a living outside the crème de la crème group of his must be avant-garde."

"Sharp-tongued, isn't she?" Binkie grinned at John, who laughed.

"I think you two have known each other too long."

"Much too long," Val agreed, sipping some of the scalding demitasse in front of her. She had ordered the Turkish coffee, enjoying the strong bitter brew in minuscule quantities.

After dinner they decided to go to Elaine's for a nightcap. When Val looked at her watch and it was one in the morning, she remembered that Dan was going to call her at eleven.

Binkie drove her home in his limousine, telling the chauffeur not to hurry.

31

"Binkie, I want him to hurry. I'm tired . . . and I should call Dan before I go to bed."

"Don't be silly, Val. He'll be sound asleep. Working out on those fields makes you tired."

Val put her head back on the plush upholstery. "So, what do you want to say to me . . . and don't bother asking how I knew. . . . When you tell Henry to drive slowly to my place, you have something to say. What is it?"

"Val, I think you should take the job in San Francisco. It's a great opportunity for you. You'll have equal billing with a man like Dean Carver who is a well-known commodity all across the country. I think you should do it."

Val turned her head to look at him. "Trevor pressuring you again?"

Binkie shrugged. "He mentioned it to me last time I was in California."

"My father wants me back in the old scene, Binkie, and I'm not going. I don't fit in with that picture anymore . . . and I am not going to marry another man just to add luster to the Rogers name or the Valley Wine Company."

"Your father is in banking, Val. It was your mother who was the wine company," Binkie instructed her.

"Thank you for keeping track of my family connections. . . . I can also remember it was Craig Gilmartin's father who owned those many acres of land that my father's firm acquired for the use of the Valley Wine Company." She held up her hand palm outward. "Don't pressure me, Bink. I half decided to go out there and look over the operation, but if you see my father before I do, please tell him I am not jumping into any grasshopper social scene to please him or Michael or Carol."

Binkie said no more, but told her he would call the next day before he left for California.

When she was undressing, she toyed with the idea of calling Dan and explaining where she was at eleven when he called, but she remembered what Binkie had said about it being late . . . that Dan would be tired.

32

She climbed between the sheets, body sore and missing Dan. She rubbed his pillow, then caught it between her hands and pressed it to her cheek. It was small comfort, but it helped her sleep.

She had the feeling the phone had been ringing many times as she struggled up from the wool of sleep. Why hadn't Mrs. Hernandes answered it? Val wondered as she blinked her eyes into focus. Then she looked at the clock. Six! No wonder. Mrs. Hernandes wouldn't arrive for a half hour yet.

"Yes?" She yawned into the receiver.

"For God's sake . . . I thought for a moment that you hadn't slept home last night," Dan barked in her ear, waking her fully.

"Dan . . . oh, Dan . . . good morning. What are you doing up so early?"

"I'm going out to practice in fifteen minutes. We're scrimmaging an all-star team for charity. Where were you last night?" There was a muffled curse. "I called three times."

"I was at dinner with Binkie. He flew into town this week and called. I was at loose ends, so I had dinner with him."

"Why didn't you call when you came home?"

"By the time I undressed it was two—"

"Two in the morning? What the hell were you doing?"

Val sat up in bed. "Now listen, Dan . . . I'm old enough to stay out at night. You're not my mother." Val took a deep breath. "I don't want to argue with you—"

"I don't want to argue with you either . . . especially since I have to tell you that I'll be down here for another week. . . ."

"Dan . . ." Val groaned into the phone. "Why? It's so lonely here without you."

"Dammit, what do you think it's like here?" Val could hear him breathe deeply. "Val, come down here . . . for a week."

33

Val hugged the phone to her, feeling her insides deflate like a pricked balloon. "Dan . . ." she swallowed. "I want to be with you . . . but I have to tape my segment with Butch Delwar today and tomorrow. . . ."

"Dammit, Val . . . I don't ask much of you . . ."

"I . . . I know that . . . I want to . . ."

"But you won't." Dan's voice was like the metal bit of a drill working on a rock.

"I can't."

"I won't ask again. So long, Val."

The buzzing in her ears finally penetrated her fog of pain, and she replaced the phone on its cradle.

That day the taping went sour, the daredevil Mr. Delwar turning into a pussycat when he was told to speak into the microphone. It took far too much time, setting her back on her routine work.

John Dewey called her to have lunch with him, but Val demurred. The combination of late hours and her disagreement with Dan had turned her zombielike, and she didn't feel up to making business chitchat over a salad.

"Then if you won't have lunch with me and I'm flying back this afternoon so I can't take you to dinner, will you just think about the proposition that CBC is offering you?" There was a pause. "Do you think you could come out and see the operation? Don't answer now. Think about it, then call me. Deal?"

"Deal."

That night Val dragged home at seven thirty at night, hoping that Mrs. Hernandes hadn't put a casserole in for her. All she wanted was a salad and a glass of milk . . . then shower and bed.

She unlocked the door and her heart sank. She smelled chicken divan, one of Dan's favorites, cooking in the kitchen.

She flipped through the small amount of mail on the side table. Bills . . . advertisements.

"Don't I even get a hello?" The deep velvet steel voice

34

was behind her, halfway up the staircase leading to the second floor.

Val whirled around, still holding some of the envelopes in her hand. "Dan. Oh, Dan, where did you come from?" Val croaked, dropping the mail and staring at him as he stood there in jeans and a silk shirt that she had given him. He looked sexy, alive . . . warm and beautiful, Val thought, before she catapulted across the room and he came down the stairs two at a time.

He swept her up in his arms, his mouth fixing to hers like a magnet to iron.

Val felt her blood begin to move and her heart begin to pump. Dan was here. He was holding her. This is what she needed. She clung to him, her arms circling that strong neck, her fingers digging into him.

When he released her mouth, they were eye to eye because Dan had lifted her up his body as he often did. "Baby, I missed you."

"Oh, I missed you. How did you know I needed you so tonight?"

"I just knew that I needed you." He put his arm under her backside so that he could hold her as he walked down the hall to the kitchen. "Mrs. Hernandes said that I was to watch the chicken and take it out in fifteen minutes. You know she won't use the microwave." Dan grinned at her, then kissed her cheek, before setting her down on the tile floor of the kitchen.

She was removing her coat, watching him as he lifted the casserole from the oven before she asked him again. "Dan, where did you come from? How did you get here?"

"Florida. Plane." He grunted, edging the hot dish onto the special section of counter for hot plates. He looked up at her grinning. "I wanted home cooking and my lady . . . not necessarily in that order."

"I should hope not." Val grinned back at him, feeling helium-light, giddy with happiness because Dan was in her orbit again. "Don't you have to play tomorrow?" Hope ballooned in her.

"Yes, I do . . . but I told Morey that if I didn't see you I wouldn't be able to handle the ball at all. When you leave for work tomorrow, I'll be taking the morning flight out of Kennedy."

"Oh, Dan . . ." Val streaked across the kitchen, not paying attention to him when he told her to watch the bread knife in his hand.

"We have tonight, my baby . . . and tonight is the beginning of forever. You won't sleep all night, angel. Will you mind? At least I'll be able to sleep on the plane." He tried to ease her back and away from the knife.

Val hurled herself at him again, grabbing at him, pulling his head down to hers, her mouth open and wanting his. At once his muscled arms enfolded her close. "So who's complaining about a lack of sleep?" Val cooed.

They fed the chicken divan to each other, sipping Blanc de Blanc with it. Neither wanted anything else . . . not even coffee.

They left the table, their arms around each other, to sit in the lounge and listen to the soaring power of Mozart.

"Even Wolfgang Amadeus can't pull my thoughts from you tonight, pet. Have I told you how empty that motel was? Even the guys began to get on my nerves. I knew if I didn't see you, I'd blow my top," Dan said into her neck as she sat on his lap and let her fingers play over his face and chest.

"I was the same way. Nothing went right," Val whispered into his ear, blowing there, feeling his heart pick up speed under her hand.

"I think I'll invent a way to shrink you down to wallet size, then I can carry you wherever I go," Dan muttered against her skin.

She felt his body harden against her with a sense of satisfaction. She needed to know that Dan wanted her, that he had to have her. It didn't mitigate her desire or

36

lessen it, but it made it more acceptable to her. When she was apart from Dan, it didn't seem possible that he could love her as much as she loved him. It embarrassed her, frightened her even, the scope of emotion that was generated by his very name. "I wish we could go away . . . just the two of us . . ." Val whispered. All at once there was an urgent flood rising in her, telling her to take Dan and run, forget the commitments, forget careers . . . run . . . with Dan . . . run.

"What are you thinking, lady mine?"

"Just that I wish we could take a trip . . . anywhere. . . ."

He leaned back from her, his eyes assessing her, examining her spirit. "You're afraid . . ." He kissed the palm of her hand. "What frightens you, babe? Don't you think I'm big enough to scare your goblins away?"

"You're big enough." Val sighed into the well-muscled neck, feeling comforted by that large body that seemed to surround her with safety. "We need more of this."

"Ummm, you're right." Dan cuddled her closer. "I suppose you're well aware of what you're doing to me."

"Yes," Val answered, delighting in the passionate body she hugged to her own.

"And you don't think we get enough, is that it?" Dan snarled, swinging his body around so that he was lying supine and Val was on top of him.

She grinned down at him, letting her hair curtain out the rest of the room. "Oh, yes, we get enough loving"— she stopped smiling—"we just need more time to talk . . . to tell each other things . . . to discuss . . ."

The phone rang, making them both scowl.

"Let it ring." Dan pulled her closer to him, his mouth teasing hers.

The phone rang twelve times before Val scrambled from the couch and reached for it where it sat on the coffee table. "Yes, he's here." Grimacing, she held the phone out to Dan.

"Yeah . . . yeah . . . listen, Morey, I said I'd be back tomorrow. If the media doesn't like it, tell them to . . . all right . . . yeah, tomorrow." Dan almost tumbled the phone to the floor, he hung up with such a crash. "Come here, woman. I'm not putting up with any more interruptions." Dan lifted her from the floor so that she was kneeling in front of him as he sat on the couch. "Could I talk you into unplugging the phone and going to bed, angel?"

"Yes . . . to both questions," Val crooned to him, pushing down the niggling thought that there was something more she was going to discuss with him. She, too, wanted no more interruptions, no more phone calls, no more outside world.

They walked up the stairs to the second floor slowly, their arms around each other, stopping on every other step to kiss and mumble love words.

That night their lovemaking even astounded them. It had always been good between them, but it was as though a new height had been reached, so that when Dan penetrated her body, he also entered her soul. It seemed that when her body embraced him, she took pieces of him to herself to become part of her. She had not been a virgin when she and Dan had first met and had not had a virgin's discomfort when they loved, but now Val felt a sharp sweetness to their loving that had her gasping, even flinching.

"God, love, I didn't hurt you, did I?" Dan pressed her along his body as though to shield her.

"No . . . it didn't hurt me . . . but it felt different, as though you were making love to me for the first time. . . ." Val felt a vague disquiet for a moment, as though her body had betrayed her and become part of Dan . . . a part that could never be returned to her. It was an unsettling moment. Her skin felt peeled back. She felt exposed and vulnerable.

They woke each other again in the night, and there was

a frenzy to their loving as though they wanted to hold back the clock.

Again Val felt vulnerable, naked. She wanted to analyze her feelings, dissect the disturbing emotions, but her eyes were too heavy. They fell asleep holding one another, the one disquieting moment still deep in Val's being.

The next morning was frantic. They had overslept even with Mrs. Hernandes calling them.

Breakfast was juice, coffee, vitamin pills.

"You can't do that," Val wailed. "It's all right for me, I'm used to it, but you should eat a big breakfast."

"Silly lady." Dan kissed her nose while he slipped into the leather vest he would wear to fly to Florida and picked up a small gym bag. Dan always traveled light.

They held each other in the taxi, making idle conversation.

Too soon, Dan was helping her from the cab, telling the driver to wait, then walking her to the employee's entrance of the studio.

Even with so many people passing back and forth, Dan lifted her up into his arms and kissed her passionately, his tongue teasing the inside of her mouth. "Bye, love. See you soon."

Val nodded, feeling tears in her throat. She rarely cried, had often seen him off somewhere, but today she felt a cold loss as she watched him return to the cab, then leave.

She stood there watching until long after the vehicle was out of sight, until her assistant Holly, just arriving for work, tapped her on the arm and asked her if she wanted to stop for coffee before going upstairs.

Val wanted nothing more than to be alone, crawl into a broom closet, and hide behind the mops. "A cup of coffee sounds fine, Holly."

Dan called her that night to tell her that he had arrived in good shape but they had some new recruits and that the team seemed to be drawing together. "It looks as though

I'll be down here for a time, honey, but I'll call you when I can."

"Fine." Val tried to mask her disappointment that he wouldn't be coming home for the weekend. "I'll miss you."

"I ache for you, babe, but at least we had last night."

"Yes." They talked for a short time longer, then broke the connection.

Val wandered around the brownstone on her own. "Maybe I should get a dog to keep me company. . . ." Val thought of her tiny backyard and discarded the idea. "Still . . . it would be nice to have a dog." She ambled to the foyer of the brownstone, looked out the side glass windows of the door to the front steps that led down to the street level. The black wrought iron lamp that was in front of their place gleamed with an eerie light in the icy rain.

A movement at the base of the street lamp caught her attention. Was that a small dog outside? Val thought. What a coincidence! She was thinking of a dog, and now one appears in front of her house. She opened the heavy steel door that had a wood look to it, the brass door knocker now glittering with drops of moisture. "Hello, doggy." Val spoke to the dark shadowy thing behind the lamp.

All at once the dark thing sprinted up her steps and vaulted into the foyer.

Openmouthed, Val closed the door, automatically turning the night lock, and swiveled to face the intruder. "Oh no . . . a cat! I hate cats." Val grimaced at the wet, bedraggled thing that she could discern as not black, but a striped silvery color, at the moment, dirty, muddy, and wild-eyed. "I suppose you bite." Val had never heard anything good about cats. She opened the door and gestured for the animal to depart. Instead it began to wash its paws.

Val closed the door again. "I don't like cats," Val reiterated, standing there, facing the wet, ragged creature. "All right, you win, it's a bad night. I'll give you some milk. . . . That's what cats like, isn't it? Then you leave. Deal?"

The silver cat paused for a moment and looked at her and blinked once.

Val stalked to the kitchen. "I don't know what Mrs. Hernandes is going to say about you tramping about her clean kitchen," Val admonished the feline, who had followed her to the kitchen and now watched the milk bottle.

When Val put down the saucer of milk, it seemed to disappear in an instant. The cat sat back and looked at her.

"Now see here. This is not a rescue mission. I don't like cats, as I have told you. . . ." Val opened the refrigerator, lifting the tops on covered dishes. She saw a piece of cooked tuna steak that was left over from last night's dinner. It had been broiled in lemon. Val didn't think the cat would eat it, but she proceeded to flake the fish with a fork, then placed it on the saucer that had held the milk.

It was gone in seconds. The cat sat down to look at her.

"See here . . . you have an appetite like Dan." Val tried to be stern, but she found the placid stare of the cat amusing. She went back to the refrigerator, found a small dish of stew, diced the meat and carrots, and gave it to the cat.

It was eaten. Then he began to wash himself again while Val rinsed out his dishes.

She tried to talk him into leaving again. He curled into a ball in the front hall and went to sleep.

Val was nonplussed. She went back to the kitchen, took some towels from the kitchen cupboard, put them on the floor, then she spread some papers nearby. "I just hope you understand the paper message and do not soil the rest of the house," she muttered to herself, then jumped as she felt something rub against her leg. She looked down at the cat who was looking up at her.

The phone rang before she could give the cat the lecture on how to be a welcome guest.

"Val? It's Binkie. Listen, I had dinner with John Dewey

41

tonight and he is very anxious to have you out here in San Francisco."

"Really?" Val answered vaguely. "Binkie, how do you train a cat?"

"What? Val, have you been drinking? Because if you have, I tell you now, you've had enough. Now you know how I hate to be a nag, but if you're seeing things, old girl, I think you should call it quits. . . ."

"Binkie, don't be a fool. A cat walked into my house . . ."

"Easy. Toss him out."

". . . and he was hungry and very tired. He's sleeping here in the kitchen."

"God, Val, are you insane; the thing's probably rabid."

"I don't think so." Val frowned into the phone.

"Well . . . anyway . . . will Dan let you come out for a few days?"

"Dan is in Florida," Val murmured, watching the cat scratch at the towels, then curl into the middle of the nest it had made.

"Good. Then you could come west for a few days, could you not?"

"What? Ah . . . perhaps I could." Val tried to concentrate on the conversation. California. Yes, maybe it would be a good idea to go out there while Dan was in Florida. That way she wouldn't miss him quite so much.

"Binkie, let me call you back . . . tomorrow. I'll let you know then."

"Come out, Val. It's the opportunity of a lifetime."

Val hung up the phone, then bent down to pet the cat, her hand just lightly touching the wet fur and lifting off when the animal yawned and opened its eyes.

She wrote a note for Mrs. Hernandes about the cat, then she went upstairs to bed.

After an hour of tossing and turning, she rose and took a hot shower. Sleep didn't come right away afterwards, but she was more relaxed so that she did sleep after a time.

42

The next morning she rose in plenty of time to shower and shampoo her hair and don the salt-and-pepper angora suit that Dan had purchased for her, the mauve and pink mixture flattering to her fair coloring.

When she went down to the morning room, Mrs. Hernandes was there pouring her coffee.

The woman smiled at Val. "The *gato,* what do you call him, eh?"

Val stared at her housekeeper for a moment, then she recalled last evening. "Oh . . . the cat. I hope he didn't make a mess in your kitchen."

"No. He was a good *gato* and used the papers. I have called the market to bring the litter for him, and I have ordered food too. What do you call the *gato?*"

"Well . . . I wasn't planning on keeping him. . . ." Val paused when she saw Mrs. Hernandes's crestfallen face. "Ah . . . you see I thought maybe I would have a dog . . ."

"*Perro* is much work." Mrs. Hernandes crossed her arms over her ample bosoms.

"I suppose. Umm . . . ah . . . perhaps he might want to go . . . to his home," Val tried.

"Not that one. He is a big boy . . . he likes it here."

"Perhaps we shouldn't take in an animal that hasn't been checked by a veterinarian . . ."

Mrs. Hernandes left the room, brought back a sectioned grapefruit and triangles of toast. "I will call the doctor today. But what will you call the *gato?*"

"What will I call . . . him? I'll just call him Gato."

## CHAPTER THREE

When Dan called her during the week and told her that it looked like a two-week stint down in Florida, she called Binkie and told him that she would be coming to California the following Monday.

It had been four days since Gato had come to live in the brownstone, and the vet had pronounced him a healthy male who took his shots like a soldier.

He no longer slept in the kitchen at night but had gotten into the habit of sleeping on a chair in Dan's and Val's bedroom.

"I don't know what Dan is going to say about you sleeping up here with us," Val told Gato the evening before she was to fly to California as she packed her bag. "Dan says you sound like a silver tabby he had once when he was a boy, and he had called him Melchior after one of the three kings of the Bible . . ." Val rambled to the cat, thinking of Dan, missing him so much that it sometimes frightened her. She kept telling herself she had to be strong. She and Dan wouldn't go on forever. For one thing he was two years younger than she. He would want a younger woman someday. Many men today preferred younger women, a voice deep inside tortured her. Dan was a very virile, handsome man in a very exciting business. He could have his choice of women.

Val threw down the hairbrush she was about to pack in her overnight bag, making Gato jump from the chair and hop onto the bed. He licked his paws and washed his face, the action making Val laugh as it always did. She couldn't believe how the animal had insinuated himself into her life. She had begun to look forward to the evenings spent with Gato on her lap while she worked out of her briefcase or talked to Dan on the telephone.

She saw in the paper that the LaRue family, part owner with Binkie of the Titans, had given a party for the members of the team. Elaine LaRue, daughter of Jake and Eugenia LaRue, was photographed with the Titans quarterback looking up into Dan's eyes. "Why aren't these women ever ugly, Gato?" Val posed the question as she happened to look at the copy of *Day* magazine open to the page with the picture on it.

Gato purred loudly, his eyes on Val, blinking in a slow rhythm.

She was in bed when Dan called that night, wanting to get some sleep because of her early rise in the morning.

"Hi, angel. I've missed you," Dan growled into the phone.

"Is that between parties . . . or all the time?" Val couldn't keep the tartness from her voice.

"I guess you saw the picture . . . you know what I've told you about those pictures . . ."

"Yes, I know what you've told me . . . but I also have a vivid imagination . . ." Val finished, petting Gato, who had left his perch on the chair to jump to her bed. "Get off the bed, I'm trying to talk," she muttered to the cat.

"Who the hell is that?" Dan barked, making the cat back away and hiss.

"It's Gato. He heard me speaking to you and decided to join our conversation."

Dan chuckled, his tones relaxed. "Damn devil, he should be down in the kitchen."

"That's what Mrs. H. says." Val turned over on her stomach, sighing with warmth and comfort.

"Are you turning on your tummy?" Dan snarled softly.

45

"Yes." Val took deep, shuddering breaths, the sound of his voice turning her to melted ice cream.

"I wish I was there to massage your back."

"You don't wish it anymore than I do." Val breathed back at him. "I wish we weren't so far apart . . . and we'll be even farther when I'm in California."

"California?" There was tension in the silence that came over the wire from Florida.

"I thought since you will be gone for at least ten more days, I would take the opportunity to go out to San Francisco now, and then we wouldn't be apart when you come home again."

"I see. I thought we would have discussed this California thing a little more before you went out there." Dan's voice was flat.

"Ah . . . yes . . . well . . . we would have if you had been here, Dan, but . . ."

"So . . . you thought you might as well go ahead with this and not mention it to me. . . ." His voice was a sledgehammer on rock.

"No . . . no. I was going to tell you . . . I'm telling you now. . . . We're discussing it now . . ." Val struggled to keep her voice from rising with the mixture of panic and anger that was frothing her insides.

"Yes . . . we're speaking of it because it just happened to come up in idle conversation. Why didn't you call me and talk this over before you said that you would go out there?"

"And what would you have said?"

"That you damn well shouldn't go until we've had a chance to talk, face-to-face."

"Well even if I had flown down to Tampa, would we have had time to talk? It seems to me that you don't have time for anything but partying . . ."

"That's a damn lie and you know it," Dan roared, making Val hold the receiver away from her ear.

"Then how is it that you make all the periodicals when they mention parties?" Val raised her voice.

"Are you going to tell me that you have not once gone out to dinner . . . or a party with your friends?" Dan grated over the wire.

"I have not gone to a party . . . but I did have dinner one evening with Binkie and—"

"Ah, yes, the ubiquitous Binkie. He's like a growth on your skin, isn't he, Val?"

"That's a nasty thing to say. Binkie and I have been friends since childhood." Val drew breath into her lungs. "I don't think this talk is getting us anywhere . . . and I do have an early flight in the morning. . . ."

"Don't let me disturb you." The phone crashed down, the sound reverberating in Val's ear.

"Damn you, damn you, Danilo Cravick, for making me feel this way," she shouted into the now buzzing phone.

Gato rose and stretched and came over to her and curled up in her lap as she sat Indian-fashion on the bed.

Val replaced the receiver with shaking fingers, hearing the clang as the sword of Damocles landed. Her hands clenched and unclenched in Gato's fur. "He . . . he's unreasonable. He never listens. He's bossy." She sniffed, swiping at her face with an edge of the sheet. "Who does he think he's pushing around? My life ran very smoothly before he entered it, and it will again." Val switched out the light, punched at her pillow, and squeezed her eyes shut. Why doesn't he call back? Why doesn't he say he's sorry and tell me he loves me? Thoughts swirled in her mind, pushing sleep away. He's never *really* said he loves me. Why can't he stay in his room and read a book instead of going to parties? I don't go to parties.

The voice of reason deep inside her was successfully squashed by the petulant questions that washed over her one after the other.

When sleep finally came, the moon was fading, and she had Gato cuddled to her side. Her last thought was of

47

herself, many years hence, alone in her bed . . . with no one but Gato.

The next day was too hectic to question whether she should take the bull by the horns and call Dan or not.

She was down in the foyer listening to Mrs. Hernandes list the things that she would be doing to keep Gato from getting too lonely when Val made up her mind to call Dan.

She was striding toward the study-library room that both she and Dan used as a hideaway when the taxi tooted outside.

Val looked from the door of the room to the front door where the taxi was honking again. "Mrs. Hernandes . . . if Mr. Dan should call please tell him . . ."

Honk! Honk! Honk!

". . . that I'll call him when I can. . . ." Val sprinted out the door to the sounds of Gato yowling behind her and the taxi driver saying, "Hey lady, you ain't the only fare I got. Besides, I don' like drivin' to Kennedy. . . ." The driver saw her into the car with her two-suiter and her overnight bag, slammed the door, and went around to his side mumbling about "dames that never know what time it is."

The flight to San Francisco was long and tiring to Val, who wasn't able to eat the plastic food that a smiling attendant wanted to serve her.

Some of the time she slept. Some of the time she read. All of the time she saw Dan's face before her eyes. It was as though his image was fitted to the front of her brain and all other activities, people, things, floated through her consciousness with all the solidity of a fog. Dan! Dan! Dan!

Seeing the skyline of San Francisco as the plane began its descent brought Val out of her torpor. The city had a beauty that had been defined in more than one song and poem, and Val was enthralled with the sight of it from the air. It was a clear day. She could see so much . . . remember so much. This city and Los Angeles had been the cities where she had grown up. She had attended schools in

48

Europe, but she had also attended Mills College in California. She felt a tug at her heart, even while she accepted that this was no longer home to her. Home was where Dan was. Home was in New York.

Landing and deplaning were done with minimum difficulty, Val not even pausing at the luggage area, since all of hers had been carryon baggage.

She was striding through the terminal when she heard her name announced on the airport loudspeaker. Going to the nearest in-terminal phone, she called the operator and was told that there was a limousine waiting for her at the south entrance to the Concourse.

Val had to laugh. She was home, all right. Nothing was ever left to chance when it came to the comfort of the elite group in which she had been allowed to move and grow as a child. "I had forgotten one of the reasons for moving to New York," Val murmured to herself as she approached the south entrance and saw a liveried chauffeur scanning the crowd. "The damned rarefied ozone we breathed had begun to strangle me." Val spoke out loud, making a passing elderly gentleman view her askance.

She strode right up to the chauffeur and faced him squarely. "I'm Valentina Gilmartin."

The man doffed his cap, inclined his head, then relieved her of the light load of her two-suiter and overnight bag. He looked behind her as though waiting for the usual dolly-load of baggage.

"Nothing else," Val announced tersely, accompanying the man outside where a light misty rain was starting. Val inhaled the damp ocean smell, filling her lungs with it.

The drive to Lombard Street, where she would be staying in the house that Binkie owned, took some time, yet it seemed to take only minutes as Val absorbed the sights and the sounds of a city she hadn't seen in seven years.

When the driver climbed the road that would take them to the top of Lombard Street, a section that only ran one way . . . down, Val looked around her with excitement.

There were changes . . . yes . . . but much of what she recalled of San Francisco was the same. The clang of the trolley made a lump rise in her throat, the hilly streets, the row houses were all a part of her childhood. It was a sweet pain.

She paid off the driver, telling him not to come up to the door with her, to continue down the corkscrew street and let her stand and look up at the turquoise door in front of her, the stone front of the house, the tiny yard, the shrubs. She had been trying to buy this house from Binkie for years . . . not because of investment but because to her it was one of the loveliest types of houses in California. Much like her brownstone in New York; oh, not as old and of different material, but the same dignity, the same true classic design that made it so quietly elegant.

"Someday that man will sell me this house." Val grinned to herself as she thought of the many arguments she had had with Binkie on the subject.

Before she could ring the bell, the door was opened, the gargoyle face of the man in front of her wreathed in smiles. "Henderson! You're still here? I don't believe it." Val grinned and grabbed the bushel-basket-sized head of the man with her one free hand and pulled it down to hers to be kissed.

"Here, Miss Rogers, let me take that for you." Elroy Henderson had once been a prizefighter; his mashed potato ears and crumpled nose attested to this. At fifty years and more he was still a big, muscular man, his limp from a fall out of a prizefight ring scarcely noticeable as he hefted her luggage and stood aside to let her pass into the two-story foyer of the House on Lombard Street, as she and Binkie always referred to it.

"Welcome home, Miss Val. It's been too long. When Mr. Binkie called, I was surprised that you were coming . . . but very glad." His lips parted in a smile. "It's many days since you were a teenager and you and Mr. Binkie came to see me fight at the Aqua Club . . ."

". . . and Binkie promised me that if I won the bet we'd made I could have one wish . . ." Val laughed at the big man at her side as they walked into the lounge that had a warming fire and lovely Indian throw rugs.

". . . and when I was the loser in the fight and you saw how bruised I was, you insisted that I have a job of your choosing, and you chose the job as butler for me at . . ."

". . . the House on Lombard Street." Val finished with a chuckle. "How Binkie hates to lose, but he has admitted that no one could keep this house better than you do." Val looked up at the tall swarthy man who looked as though he would have been more at home on a fishing boat than buttling for a fine house in San Francisco. "Do you think I have a chance of talking him out of this house this time around, Henderson?"

He shrugged, leaving the room for a moment and coming back with a tea trolley he pushed in front of him. He had poured her a cup of the fragrant brew before he answered. "I think he doesn't want this house. He never stays here . . . but because you want it, he digs in his heels."

"You know Binkie." Val nodded, then sipped. "Umm, this tea is just what I needed." She leaned back against the cushions of the Victorian settee and gestured to Henderson to sit opposite her.

When she was married to Craig and living in Los Angeles, she used to stay at this house whenever she came to town to see the opera or a show. She and Henderson had often talked long and companionably on many subjects.

He sat opposite her, looking incongruous on the love seat. He was at ease as he poured a cup of tea for himself and asked her about what she was going to do in San Francisco.

"I'm out here to see about a job. If I take it, I'm going to tell Binkie that he has to throw in the house." Val smiled at the man sitting opposite her.

51

"Good." Henderson looked around him, pride in his gaze. "I've been here twelve years, and I think it looks better now than when I started."

"I agree." Val asked him questions about his family, who lived farther north in the grape-growing Napa Valley. Henderson had been married once, but both his wife and newborn child had died soon after the birth of the child. He still had a mother and brother there. He had been a loner, down and out, broke, and a drunk, willing to take twenty-five bucks to have his head busted by any up-and-coming boxer who needed to try his talents.

It was during one of these exhibitions that Val had witnessed the battering Henderson took to the cheers of the crowd. Val, who had attended with her brother and Binkie, had never forgotten the loud hurrahs of the onlookers as Henderson's face had split like a grape and turned scarlet with blood.

"Mr. Binkie left a message that he would pick you up for dinner this evening—" Henderson began.

"Lose the message, and when he calls put him off. I don't want to go anywhere tonight." Val placed her cup with great care in the saucer, noticing the fine sediment of tea leaves that made a pattern on the bottom of her cup.

"I'll tell him that you are suffering from jet lag and need your sleep," Henderson announced.

"Jet lag? From New York? Binkie won't buy it." Val stretched and covered her mouth with one hand to mask a yawn.

"I assure you, Miss Rogers, he will buy it." Henderson never called her Mrs. Gilmartin . . . always Miss Rogers.

"I think I will go up and shower some of this grime away." Val rose from the couch, Henderson already on his feet.

"Do that, miss. I'll have your clothes pressed for you. There is lingerie in the drawers, there is a robe, there are jeans . . ."

Val nodded her head, hearing Henderson but not really

comprehending. She was bone-tired. She pushed open the door at the top of the winding stairway leading to the upper hall. She had always slept in the bedroom that overlooked the fenced-in garden behind the house.

She gazed about her, a vague pleasure assailing her that the rose and gold bedroom with the wall-to-wall Persian rug in rose and gold was much the same. The paint had been freshened, she could tell, but the crocheted bedspread in rose color was much the same, the brass-backed bed was still king-sized, and on a dais, the curtains were still swagged-back rose silk with rose and gold floral patterned shades on an ecru background. It was warm and restful.

Val sighed and stripped the clothes from her back. Would Dan call her tonight? He should. He had been abrupt and short with her and hung up the phone on her.

The shower was like a water massage. Much of her tension was being washed away.

She slipped into a hot pink dressing gown after drying her shampooed hair, then walked through to the bedroom and fell onto the bed face downward.

She had no idea of the time when she woke, except that it was dark. She felt rested.

Rising, she went to the dressing room off the bedroom, which was nothing more than a narrow corridor with wall-to-ceiling drawers, a walk-in closet, and a vanity with lights all around the mirror, drawers for makeup and even a jewelry case. She snapped open the case and stared down at the many things she had almost forgotten she owned, things her father and Craig had given her: gold, platinum, a variety of gems, all extremely valuable, all unnecessary to her well-being.

She pulled open a small cupboard and extracted a pair of designer jeans in gold velvet, pairing it with a frilly cream-colored satin blouse and Turkish slippers of soft supple suede.

When she went down to dine, she could smell lemon

sole, her favorite. She stopped on the fifth step from the bottom of the staircase, pressing her hand to her abdomen. Her stomach felt queasy . . . from the trip, no doubt, Val thought.

Henderson came through from the kitchen when she reached the foyer. "Mr. Binkie has been well and truly put off, miss. Shall I serve your dinner in the morning room instead of the dining room?"

"Please . . . and will you join me for dinner?" She smiled when she saw the slight frown on his much-abused face. "Please. You know how I enjoy our talks, Henderson."

"Of course." Henderson grinned at her, his one missing tooth in the front a comforting sight for Val. She only saw the hole where the tooth had once been when he smiled.

At dinner, Val drank gallons of seltzer water and lime, finding the smell of the sole too much for her travel-weary stomach. She ate three rolls and the mashed potato, none of the salad, tea instead of coffee, and two helpings of linzer torte that Henderson had made from a Viennese recipe . . . or so he told Val.

"No, I don't think I want any liqueur, Henderson. I'll just have more tea. Come into the lounge with me and we'll listen to some music."

Henderson watched her for long moments, then nodded.

When the strains of Mozart filled the room, Val was frozen to her seat. Then she jumped up, stopped the record player, and turned on the stereo FM station with popular music. "Not a night for the classics," Val explained lamely to a watchful Henderson.

They talked. Val saw his lips move and felt her jaw go up and down . . . so she knew that they talked, although she would not have been able to recall one single topic that they discussed, even if she'd been asked to only a few moments later.

She was willing the phone to ring. Dan would call. He would call.

She went to bed after a long hot soak in the tub.

When there was a knock at her door just after she'd gotten under the covers, she shot to a sitting position, turned on the light, and called "enter." No doubt she hadn't heard the phone, and Henderson was coming to tell her that there was a call from Dan for her.

He walked into the room balancing a steaming cup on a tray. "I thought you might like some lemon and honey before you try to sleep." His voice was expressionless, but Val knew he saw the tremor in her hand when she took the cup from him. He waited by the side of the bed while she drank the steaming tart, sweet liquid.

"Thank you." Val swallowed to clear her throat of its huskiness. She swallowed again, feeling a heartburn from the hot drink. She never had indigestion. She must have had more jet lag than she thought possible.

"Good night, miss." Henderson took the tray and left the room, closing the door quietly.

"Good night . . ." Val pressed her closed fist against her chest, burping gently.

She tossed and turned for a long span of time, getting up at intervals to go to the bathroom. When she looked at the bedside clock, blinking at the two-in-the-morning time, she still wished that Dan would call her.

The next day she rose feeling as woolly-headed and foggy as the San Francisco day. She raised the shade and looked out into the misty backyard with a sigh. She felt tired, washed out . . . but hungry.

While she was breakfasting on eggs and kippers, the queasiness, the heartburn, came back. Val pushed back her plate and took a sip of her fresh-squeezed orange juice. It had a metallic taste. She grimaced and picked up the morning newspaper.

As was her custom since meeting Dan, she turned to the sports page first, and there was Dan on the field being sacked by two burly players, his arm still back to throw the football. The headline read, "CRAVICK . . . ALL-TIME

GREAT . . . LOSING HIS TIMING? SACKED THREE TIMES IN
SCRIMMAGE GAME."

Val held the picture in front of her in rigid concentration, her insides knotting as she thought of the pummeling Dan was taking. She jumped when Henderson spoke to her.

"I didn't mean to startle you, miss. Mr. Binkie is on the phone. Shall I . . ."

"I'll take it here," Val told him, her mouth feeling chalky, her lips dry. She watched him plug the phone into the wall and hand it to her. "Thank you." She took a shuddering breath, her one hand in protective covering on Dan's picture. "Binkie?"

"Val. Why the hell didn't you call me?"

"I was sleeping."

"Jet lag. That's what that hoodlum Henderson told me. What crap that is. You've never had jet lag on that trip before. Your problem is spending too much time in New York. The air has poisoned you. When you get out here to Sweet California, your lungs can't handle it."

"Thank you, Doctor Poop," Val sighed into the phone.

"What's the matter with you? Never mind. I don't want you giving me a song and dance about Cravick. . . ."

Stung, she straightened from her slouched position in the chair, forgetting that her breakfast was sitting like a lump in chest. "You will kindly keep your opinions of Dan to yourself."

"All right, all right . . ." Binkie soothed her, backing down as he always had when Val's temper began to simmer.

"Is your office still off the Embarcadero in the Twin Towers Building?"

"Yes. Can you be here at ten?"

"Yes." Val didn't slam down the receiver, but she cut the connection quickly, angry at Binkie . . . angry at herself for getting angry at Binkie because he guessed why she was feeling under par. Damn Dan Cravick! If he didn't

56

want to call her, that was fine with her. She wouldn't pine away!

Why don't you call him? a small voice whispered deep inside of her.

"Never," Val snapped, surging to her feet and rocking the coffee cup on the table in front of her.

"Miss?" Henderson poked his head through from the kitchen. "Was there something that you wanted?"

"No. I'm going downtown to meet Binkie. Does he still have a car here?"

"Yes. Would you like me to drive you, miss? The streets have changed somewhat; the parking is tricky near the Towers." Henderson stepped fully into the morning room and watched her.

Val stared out the window at the wisps of mist being chased away by breezes and strengthening sunlight. "The cable cars. Do they still run by Lombard Street?"

"Yes . . . if you get off at . . ." Henderson went to the sideboard opened up a drawer, showed her a schedule and the through street where she would alight for the short two-block walk up the hill to the Twin Towers where Binkie's office was located and the CBC affiliate station where she would be interviewed. For a moment she wished that Binkie didn't have his hand in this pie. A strange goose-bumpy sensation ran over her skin. Was her father involved with the CBC affiliate?

She paused for a moment in donning the gold and brown tweed suit of finest wool, the Chanel jacket enhanced by the frilly jabot of the cream silk blouse. No. Trevor Rogers had his money and fingers in many pies, but she had yet to hear that he and Binkie had ever teamed up in a financial venture.

She looked at herself in the mirror, the medium pumps in camel-colored calf matching the shoulder strap briefcase she carried in lieu of purse. Her hat was a gold Australian fedora with a pheasant feather in brown and gold on the flat side of the hat. "You'll do," she told her mirror image. "Even if Dan said you look like an Aussie soldier in the hat." She grimaced at the mirror, swung her briefcase to her shoulder, and grabbed some change off the dresser top before she went downstairs to Henderson.

The cable car was the same as she had remembered. At first she was content to swing from a strap, but then she took a seat, discovering that she could see more on either side of the street. She had forgotten how chilly one could get in a cable car, and she was glad for her wool suit. She didn't bother to unzip her foldaway umbrella from the bottom of her briefcase when she alighted from the car, content to let what was left of the mist strike her face. She inhaled the fresh moist air and started up the hill to the Twin Towers Building.

She was sorry to arrive so soon. There were so many new things to see in the Cultural Capital of the West, as her father referred to San Francisco.

She took one last look around before she entered the glass and chrome towers. She was walking toward the printed office directory when she heard her name called.

"For God's sake, Val, what kept you?" Binkie looked surly. "I've been waiting here for hours . . ."

"Minutes, probably." Val laughed at her frowning childhood friend. "Are we going up to your office or right to the studio?"

"The studio." Binkie was short with her, leading the way to a bank of elevators and punching the button board of the last one. "This is their own elevator . . . takes us right to the reception area."

Their swift rise to the twentieth floor was in silence, Binkie still miffed, Val uncaring.

All at once she wanted to push the button to take her to the lobby, run from the building, go back to Lombard Street, take her bags, and fly back to New York . . . or maybe to Tampa. She didn't want to be here. Why was she here? What would Dan say if she suddenly surprised him in Tampa? He'd probably laugh and say that he knew that she would come around to his way of thinking sooner or later.

Spurred on by the thought, she marched from the elevator head high, toward the reception desk. "I'm Valentina Gilmartin," she announced to the receptionist for the CBC affiliate SOFM.

She was happy to see John Dewey and was glad of both his and Binkie's support when the interview proceeded. They weren't even halfway through when Val sensed that she was accepted in the eyes of the persons sitting around the table with her.

She had dinner with Binkie and John that night, elated with her success, but still not committing herself to a contract with SOFM.

That night she slept long and deeply.

The next night she called Dan in Tampa.

"Hello? Who is this? Could you speak up please? There's a party going on here. Yes, this is Dan Cravick's suite. This is Elaine LaRue speaking."

Val licked her dry lips. "This is Valentina Gilmartin . . ."

"Sorry . . . this must be a bad connection. Maybe you could call back tomorrow."

Val stared into the buzzing phone in her hand, a coldness filling her. She replaced the phone on the cradle carefully, then picked it up again and dialed. "John? Yes, this is Val. I think I'd like to take you up on that trial run deal. I do have about a month's vacation coming to me. . . ."

"Val, that's great. You won't regret it."

Val tried to smile into the phone, but her face hurt. "I don't think I will either. In fact I think it will be good for me to be back home in California."

"Ah . . . Val . . . I was wondering if I could take you out to dinner tomorrow night. I know this is terribly short notice . . ."

"Not at all. I'd love to go out tomorrow." Val thought

that would be the thing to do . . . chase the blues away with some pleasant company.

"I know you like classical music. *Madame Butterfly* is at the opera house. What do you think of that?"

"I love Puccini." They fixed an appropriate time and Val hung up again, her hands going up to her face, rubbing it, trying to bring some life back to a body that seemed to be dying by inches.

She jumped to her feet. "Stop that. You'll live. You've known for sometime that you and Dan were growing apart . . . little by little."

That night the dinner Henderson served her tasted like sawdust.

She went to bed to lie there staring up at the ceiling as though the dancing streak of moonlight would tell her what to do with her life. "I am damn well not going to live with heartburn just because Dan Cravick has found himself another woman. *Women*, for that matter. I can live . . . and be comfortable too." She sat up in the darkened room, pressing her fist to the dull burning sensation in her chest.

The next day she was shown to a desk at SOFM that already had her nameplate in gold sitting in one corner. The cubicle could have hardly been called an office, but there was a measure of privacy, and the desk outside with a smiling fresh-faced girl called Jane typing away at an industrious pace provided a further barrier.

It was frantic, confusing, and new, but when she sat in on the first program with Dean Carver, they meshed as though they had worked together for years. His brash, almost insolent approach to interviewing was balanced by her cool, precise, yet friendly type of questioning. The guest thanked them both for an exhilarating experience.

"You'll do, my girl." Dean Carver chewed on his unlit pipe. He saw her eying it, pulled it from his mouth, and jabbed at the air with it. "Never smoked a pipe in my life . . . but . . . I'm trying to kick cigarettes. Need to have something to put from hand to mouth and back again. Addicts have it tough."

Val laughed at his mischievous grin, then went back to her own office. "Jane, I don't want to be disturbed. I have copy to finish."

"Right."

An hour later Jane poked her head in the office. "That's the third time I've told a Dan Cravick you weren't in. His language was blue. I don't think he'll call again . . . but . . . if he does, will you talk to him?"

"Yes," Val whispered, her throat tight.

# CHAPTER FOUR

That night she worked until long past the usual time, dreading but hoping for Dan's call.

When she realized that she would be late for her dinner date with John Dewey, she left the office and took public transportation to Lombard Street, not calling Henderson to come and pick her up as he told her each morning that he would be glad to do.

She hurried through dressing, donning the two-piece silk suit in plum color, the silk blouse a shade deeper than the suit. She chose the garnet pieces of jewelry that Dan had given her, the crescent-shaped earrings fitting along the outer edge of each ear, and a pin in the shape of an orchid at the tie of her blouse. Her stockings were a pale wine color in the sheerest silklike material, her shoes and bag deep burgundy leather.

She was coming down the stairs to greet John, who was waiting for her in the foyer. When the phone rang while she was still on the stair, she gestured to John to take the call.

"No . . . this isn't Henderson. This is John Dewey, a friend of Mrs. Gilmartin's. Who's calling? Dan Cravick . . ." John covered the mouthpiece and raised an eyebrow in inquiry to her.

"I . . . I'll take it in the study." Val cleared her throat. Why couldn't she have talked to him today in work? She cursed herself for ever giving Jane the order not to disturb her; she cursed the girl for taking her so literally.

She didn't look back at John Dewey as she entered the study off the front hall and closed the door behind her. She took a deep breath, walked to the desk in the center of the room, and lifted the phone. "Hello, Dan. How are you?" How stiff she sounded even to her own ears.

"Hi. It's tough to get you." He bit off the words.

"Bad communication all around," Val snapped back, then put her free hand to her forehead, massaging there, knowing that wasn't what she had intended to say.

"What the hell does that mean?"

"It means that I'll try not to call you in the middle of a party next time . . . then maybe I won't have Elaine LaRue hanging up on me."

"What? You called last Wednesday? I never knew. Listen, Val, you know I would have returned your call. I wanted you to call."

"You should have told Elaine that." Val coughed trying to get the hoarseness from her voice.

"It was business . . . that's all. It seemed better to have a cocktail party . . ."

"Of course. I know how those things go."

"Damn you, Val. I've told you how this business is. Besides, my uncles were in town with my mother, and they wanted to meet with the owners of the Titans . . ."

"You had your mother and uncles to meet the LaRues?" Val could hear the shrill note in her voice as she posed the question.

"Yes. It was business—"

"Who the hell do you think you're fooling?" All Val's heartburn and headache seemed to intensify with every word. Her upset stomach did a fancy dive to her shoes and back, the ache between her eyes throbbing.

"No one." Dan roared back. "And who the hell do you think you're talking to? And for that matter, who the hell was the man who answered your phone?" He bellowed, blowing telephone cable to the ground cross-country, Val was sure.

"The man who is taking me to dinner, that's who." Val slammed down the phone, then covered her mouth with her hand as she started to gag. She made it to the powder room off the study and lost the cup of tea she had sipped while dressing. Dan Cravick had a terrible effect on her. Val's shaking hand wiped her mouth, then she rinsed it out with mouthwash from the cabinet, freshened her lip gloss, and left the powder room.

She had crossed the study to the door when the phone rang again. She left the study, signaling to John in the foyer not to answer. "We'll let Henderson take care of it." She smiled at John, jumped at the ring of the phone, then let him lead her from the house to his car waiting at the curb, the wheels turned into the curb as any driver in San Francisco would do.

She could no longer hear the phone ringing in the confines of the car, but she had the feeling that sulfur and steam were now coming out of the windows of the House on Lombard Street.

The restaurant was on Fisherman's Wharf, and though not fancy to look at outside, the food within was everything that John had said it would be.

"Little by little a quiet grandness is returning to the wharf. It's always been a place to visit for tourists and is getting better." There was pride in his voice. "When other cities are falling apart, San Francisco just gets better and better."

Val smiled, encouraging him to talk of the strong Italian influence of the fishermen, the pride of the artistic colony, the plethora of excellent places to dine from sidewalk carts to elegant cuisine by candlelight.

"You paint a new picture for me," Val told him. "I once lived here in San Francisco . . . and in Los Angeles . . . but I don't think I saw it quite the way you paint it.

Tell me more." Val leaned her chin on her hands and listened.

The evening sped by, and when John asked her if she would accompany him to dinner again, she looked at him as they drove home. "John, I enjoyed this evening . . . but . . . I have to tell you that I have no interest in being anything more than friends with anyone right now."

"Life crisis?"

"You could call it that," Val gulped.

"The man who called you before we went out?"

"Yes . . . but I don't want to discuss it."

"Of course." He stopped the car, pulling on the hand brake and cramping the wheels, then turned to look at her. "I'd still like to take you out again."

"Fine."

John accompanied her to the door, then bade her good night.

Days turned into weeks for Val as she delighted more and more in the job. She and Dean Carver gained momentum as a team.

She called her studio in New York and explained that though her contract was coming up for renewal and that she liked the station, she wanted to try her wings with Dean Carver for a while. There was some opposition, but in the end Val had a reluctant okay to stay with SOFM for a stint as cohost on the talk show.

Three weeks after her arrival, her father called her. "Valentina? About time you came west. Binkie tells me you're staying."

"For a while," Val responded, listening to every nuance in her father's voice. "Fly up one evening for dinner."

"Ah-huh. Good. Michael and Carol will be coming with me . . . and Les and Ruth, I suppose."

"They are married to Michael and Carol, Father," Val pointed out dryly, conscious again that it was only the wealth and family background of her brother-in-law and sister-in-law that had made them acceptable to Trevor Rogers, not Les and Ruth themselves.

"True. It's time you found someone to share your life . . . as Carol and Michael have." Trevor shot his first spear.

"Stop it, Father. If you want to come to my home and have dinner—"

"That is still Binkie Lawler's house, I believe," Trevor interrupted. "Is he staying there with you?"

". . . and have dinner . . ." Val gritted, ". . . then you had better accept that I will be making any and all decisions relating to my life."

"Binkie says that you've broken it off with that football player . . ."

"Binkie knows nothing about my life . . . and . . . Father, if this is the way you'll be questioning me . . . then perhaps it would just as well . . ."

"Fine . . . fine, I'll say nothing. We'll be there at six o'clock on Thursday evening."

"Fine. I should be home about seven thirty . . ."

"You can't be home any earlier? I own some shares in SOFM . . ."

"Damn! If I had known that, Father, I would not have worked for them."

"I take it you're telling me not to call Vance and . . ."

"Right. Good-bye, Father."

When Val replaced the receiver, she had to take long moments to compose herself. He was just the same domineering man he had always been! How could she have forgotten that! Poor Carol and Michael . . . still under Trevor Roger's thumb. Val was the oldest and could still remember how cowed her mother had been, how as a child, she had promised herself that no man would ever push her around like that. "Not to worry, Val. *You* won't have a man in your orbit at all." Val stood, walking away from the phone in the study to stare out the floor-to-ceiling windows at misty Lombard Street. It was sorrowful and solitary; a feeling of being all alone on the planet as she watched the fog close in on the hill. That's what her future would be . . . solitary, lonely. She knew deep down that no matter how many other men she met or socialized with, there would be no other man who would ever be her love.

Loneliness filled her like a bitter flood.

She turned from the window, letting the curtain fall into place, and strode back to the phone, dialing quickly. "Binkie? Two things. I want to buy this house. No . . . I'm not going to listen to you. Just draw up the papers. Yes. And one more thing. Stop going to my father with tidbits on my life. You know nothing about my private life and I resent you gossiping to my father. Yes, I said gossiping."

"Dammit, Val. I thought we were friends. Friends don't talk the way you're talking to me."

"Then stop interfering where you don't belong. I do not do it to you."

There was a long pause. "All right, Val. You win. And you can have the damn house and Henderson with it. I never quite trusted the man anyway."

"That's because when you pumped him about me, he ignored you," Val said bluntly.

"Valentina, sometimes you do border on the crass. You would do well to rid yourself of such a propensity, my girl."

"Don't get pompous with me, Binkie. This is the kid who beat you in the steeplechase at Green Meadows, in case you've forgotten."

"Damned tomboy." Binkie inhaled. "Stop chortling. You sound like a donkey with asthma."

"Come to dinner next Thursday. Father *en famille* will be the guests of honor. I need bolstering."

"From a gossip?" Binkie shot back.

"Be there, chum." Val hung up on the phone on his sputterings.

The next day she rushed to the toilet bowl on rising as

67

she had been doing almost since she arrived in California. "That's it, Val," she gasped to herself as she sat on the floor of the tile bathroom. "Your heartburn and headaches have a reason." Val felt dazed as she walked back into her bedroom and dialed New York. Myrna Deitz might have finished with her hospital rounds and be back in her office by now. After all, it was eleven in the morning back there. She sat there waiting for the call to be completed, her mind in turmoil. She had forgotten all about trying to get pregnant. It hadn't entered her mind for weeks, not since she and Dan . . . "Oh, God . . ." Val moaned.

"Hello? Hello, this is Dr. Deitz's office. Yes, one moment please."

"Val? How are you? What's new? How do you like California?"

Val got by the pleasantries, dreading asking Myrna for the name of a gynecologist, worrying about the choices she would have to make, when all at once it hit her. She was having Dan's child! Nothing in the world could be more important than that. The world could wait! She would have a part of Dan forever. Tears clogged her throat. She, who hardly ever cried, felt as though she could have filled San Francisco Bay with her tears.

"Yes, of course I know a fine woman ob-gyn in that area. You'll go a long way before you could find better than Wendy Cross. I'll buzz Lenona to give you the address and phone number. Good luck to you and Dan and call me if you need me."

"Thank you." Val didn't bother mentioning that she and Dan were no longer together. She phoned for an appointment for the next day with Dr. Cross.

The Powell Hyde cable car took her down most of the way to the medical center where Dr. Wendy Cross's office was located.

After the examination, Val sat in front of the doctor's desk twisting her hands together, the palms slippery with perspiration.

Dr. Cross looked up from where she was writing in a folder. "Well, Mrs. Gilmartin, you look fine. I think vitamin therapy is in order . . . you are a bit too slender . . . and your blood is slightly down, but all in all you are in excellent shape to deliver a child about the middle of January, I should say. . . ."

Super Bowl time! Val thought. Dan would be too busy even if he was going to take part in the parenting of this child. She mentally shrugged. It was just as well that she would be having this child by herself. She barely heard the doctor as she expounded on theories of child delivery and care.

"I think I would prefer the natural childbirth . . . it would be better for the child. Exercise, vitamins . . ." Val paused breathless, excited.

She left the office walking on air, purchased some spumoni at a small ice cream shop, and ambled to the stop where she would get the cable car for home.

She was finishing the last of her spumoni, was wiping her hands on the napkin the vendor had given her, and just about to toss the paper in the trash receptacle on the street, when it struck her. "No . . . that can't be . . ." She had spoken out loud. A woman passerby stared at her for a second. Dr. Cross had said January! She must be mistaken, Val thought, counting on her fingers. January must be a mistake! She pressed her hand to her already rounding abdomen. She had thought she was showing quite a bit for two months. She was three months pregnant. How could that be? She hadn't even thought about getting pregnant until a month after that. Hadn't she been taking her pills? Her brow wrinkled in thought. Had she forgotten or run out that one time?

"Hey, lady, did you want this car?" A man called to her as he was getting aboard the cable car. It had arrived without Val noticing it.

"Yes . . . thank you . . ." Val climbed aboard smiling

69

at the many people that smiled at her. That part of San Francisco hadn't changed. The people were still friendly.

For the entire ride, her mind tumbled and fretted trying to remember if she had not been taking her pills back in April. "I think I was," she muttered to herself as she departed the cable car, waving at the man who had told her she was missing her ride.

She walked slowly up Lombard looking around her but not seeing the profusion of flowers and the charming houses that were the pride of the city. "Somehow you goofed, Valentina." She shrugged her shoulders. "Why should I worry? I have what I want." Not everything you want, a voice inside reminded her. Dan! Dan! Dan!

Henderson met her at the door. "You look tired. You should have let me drive you wherever you were going." He scolded her, his gnarled features making him look more like a gargoyle when he frowned.

She turned to look at him when he followed her into the study. "I think a salad would be all I want tonight. I think I'm going to bed early."

Henderson nodded. "Mr. Dewey called. Jane, your secretary, called to remind you about the early-bird meeting scheduled with Mr. Carver and Mr. Dewey."

Val groaned. "I had forgotten. I'll skip breakfast tomorrow, Henderson. I have to be downtown early."

She was in bed and nodding off when the buzzer on her phone brought her fully awake. "Yes?"

"Were you asleep, Val?"

"Dan? Is it you, Dan?" Val sat upright, pressing her fist to her mouth to keep herself from crying like a baby and begging him to come out to San Francisco and get her and take her home.

"How are you? I'm sorry to waken you. . . ."

"That's all right . . . just fine . . ." Val babbled, words running round her head like marbles on a tile floor. "Is it warm in Florida?"

"I'm back in New York. We've started training at the university here. . . . I mentioned it to you . . ."

"Yes . . . yes, you did. How is training?" Val pressed the receiver tight to her ear so that she could hear Dan breathing.

"As always . . . I'm more out of shape than I think I am." He gave a harsh laugh.

"Be careful . . ." Val had visions of his shoulder and the agony she had seen on his face when the doctors worked on him in the emergency room. He hadn't known she was there and cursed roundly and steadily while the physicians had worked on him. "You've even told me that it's when you're out of shape that you can be hurt the most."

"I'm not that bad." Dan's voice had a coldness to it.

"I didn't mean . . . that you . . . well, don't get hurt."

"I won't."

There was a long silence. Val kept saying in her mind, Don't hang up, don't hang up.

"Say . . . Val . . . this cat, Gato . . ."

"Yes . . ." Val was eager to talk of anything that kept them from arguing. "Is he driving you crazy?"

"No. I like him. He's smart . . . but you should see him. He's getting fat. Every day Mrs. H. brushes him, and every night he comes up to our room. . . ." Dan's voice trailed. "I . . . ah . . . didn't know if you wanted me to stay at the brownstone . . . so . . . I thought I'd call you and see if you would like me to stay here to keep the cat company until you come back . . . to visit, then I could move back to my own place." Dan's voice was formal and correct.

The coldness that settled over Val's body was an icy fog that congealed her blood, slowed her breathing, constricted her lungs. Dan was leaving her! No, Dan had left her! "That sounds like a good plan." Her voice had a detached air to it that surprised her. How amazing that she could sound so offhand while her insides were being dealt the death of a thousand cuts.

"Val . . . I never knew you liked cats," Dan stated.

"Ah . . . I never did . . . I looked out the door one rainy night and thought I saw a dog there. When I opened the door, Gato ran in the house and wouldn't leave."

Dan laughed. "Cats are smart."

"I never knew that until he arrived. Did he have any after-effects from his altering?"

"I don't think so. . . . But I'm glad I didn't have to take him for that," Dan shuddered into the phone.

"Macho man." Val could feel the tears of good-bye on her cheeks even as she laughed.

"Not usually . . . but about altering males . . . well . . ." Dan chuckled.

"This call must be costing you a fortune." All at once Val wanted to be off the phone. She was crying hard now. God, she never cried. Pregnancy was caving in all her barriers.

"I can afford it. What is it, Val? Do you have a cold?"

"Ah . . . yes . . . I need my sleep and all that."

"Don't let me keep you. Good-bye, Val."

"Good-bye . . . good-bye . . . good-bye . . . my darling Dan . . ." Val sobbed into her pillow, her face still wet when at last she fell asleep.

She was sick the next morning as usual, but Henderson had tea and toast for her when she returned from the bathroom, his face wooden as he watched her walk slowly back into the bedroom.

"I come from a big family. My mother always recommended this treatment. My wife used it also."

"Thank you, my friend." Val sipped the tea and nibbled the dry toast, feeling her unsettled stomach relax.

"I will be driving you to work and picking you up. And there will be no argument about it." Henderson took the empty plate that had held her toast, refilled her cup, and turned toward the door.

"Tyrant."

"And don't you forget it, Miss Val."

72

The early-bird conference was a shooting and stabbing match as both factions, the conservative hold-the-line-on-spending group lined up against the you-have-to-spend-money-to-make-money contingent. Val doodled and offered an opinion only when asked.

The week went fast, and though Val was working hard, she made a conscious effort to eat better and exercise judiciously. She and Henderson had begun a regimen of walking and swimming every morning that was having a good effect on Val. Her queasiness, though still with her, was being held in control by tea and dry toast in the morning. Then she and Henderson would walk one mile to a nearby health club which they had both joined. Once there, they would swim their laps, shower, change, and walk back to the house to breakfast on something light.

"I still think that I should pay my own membership," Henderson said as they were in sight of the house on Lombard after returning from the club.

Val looked up at the burly man at her side. "Stop arguing or I'll uncork my right hook." This man had kept her from insanity, she was sure.

"Left hook." Henderson's battered lips pulled back from his teeth in a smile, the space there quite prominent.

"Mine is a right hook, more dangerous." Val followed him into the kitchen, unlacing her running shoes and sitting down in a chair to drink the tomato juice topped with a sprinkling of fresh-grated black pepper.

"Now, here is your lunch for today. Some cheese, an apple, and two thin slices of my homemade bread, lightly buttered." Henderson patted the bag on the counter as he sliced bananas on her small cup of whole grain cereal. It was all the food she could manage in the morning.

"Did you remember that my father and family are coming for dinner tonight?" Val had come back downstairs after dressing in a deep-gold cotton suit with low-heeled pumps in the same color and fabric and her usual briefcase instead of purse. She put her lunch into her briefcase carefully so as not to squash it and let Henderson lead her to the car.

"Yes." He answered her as he maneuvered the car down the corkscrew street. "We're having broiled tuna steaks, spinach salad, and Neapolitan bombe." Henderson wheeled through the morning traffic with all the chutzpah of a kamikaze pilot on a mission.

The day was crazy. The morning interview went well and almost too smooth . . . but in the afternoon the world blew up when Dean insisted that he would not interview Scott Arbel, the controversial advocate for strip mining in the farming sections of California.

"No way, Val. I won't have that man on the show. I might punch him in the nose." Dean thrust out his chin.

Val sighed and nodded, not sure she would be able to keep her cool with the obnoxious Mr. Arbel.

Finally, at shortly before seven that evening, she left the studio, with Dean promising another candidate.

Val collapsed into the back of the car as Henderson pulled into the mainstream of traffic. "I suppose they are there," she muttered tiredly.

"Yes . . . but I already told them that dinner wouldn't be served until you'd had your shower."

Val's eyes snapped open as she laughed. "You didn't? Oh Lord, I wish I could have seen that."

"Mr. Trevor took it well. He just mutters and glares at me when I go into the room."

Val laughed, feeling some of the tension leave her. Henderson was there! What could her father do? Poor Carol and Michael. How had they fared over the years? The cards and scattered letters plus the few phone calls hadn't told her much, but she assumed that they were suffering the same pressures that her father had turned on her when she was at home.

She alighted from the car and took the elevator from the garage to the second floor, deciding against greeting her father until she had showered and donned the silk hostess pajamas in antique gold and low Turkish slippers that she would wear. With the outfit she wore the topazes that Dan had given her and let her hair hang long and free like a platinum curtain down her back.

She descended the stairs to the first floor foyer, pausing to take a deep breath before turning the handle on the door to the lounge and pausing on the threshold, her eyes going at once to her father, then to her brother and sister. "Hi, everybody."

"About time." Her father walked toward her, his needle-sharp brown eyes going over her, making Val unconsciously pull in her stomach. He kissed her on both cheeks. "Still tall, too thin, too blond. Dye it?"

"No, Father." Val smiled, pleased she was no longer as sensitive to his usual barbs as she once was. Surprised, she discovered she was perfectly relaxed as she went forward to greet her sister Carol.

"Now you've got it," Carol whispered. "That's how we've handled him for years. Just smile."

Val leaned back from her younger sister, looking from her snapping brown eyes so like Trevor Rogers's to the light brown of Michael's that were more like Val's and their mother's.

Michael winked at her. "Don't look so surprised. Did you think we'd learned nothing from mother? That's the way she handled him."

Val chuckled. "You're right. I guess I never waited around long enough to toughen up."

"That plus the fact that you were so beautiful and smart that he felt threatened by you." Michael leaned down to kiss her cheek, laughing at her mouth that had dropped open in surprise. "I guess you didn't know that." He took her arm and led her across to the fireplace where a slightly heavier Ruth stood waiting, her soft smile just the same. "If he ever guessed that I loved my wife and didn't just think of her as a parcel of land for the company, he'd have a stroke," Michael drawled.

"Stop that." Ruth tapped his arm as it went round her waist. "How are you, Val? You're just as beautiful as you always were."

"And so are you." Val meant it as she looked from Michael to Ruth. "You are so happy."

"So are we." Carol came up behind Val with Les, his brown thinning hair, owl glasses, and easy smile lending no hint to his sharp accountant's mind. "Father doesn't know about Les and me either. Sometimes it's a chore to pretend coldness to each other."

"It's easier than beating her up in front of her father . . ." Les lifted one shoulder. "She hits me back."

"Come here and eat some of these canapes, Michael," Trevor Rogers commanded his only son. He looked up as Henderson entered the room again. "We don't need you here. Come back when we ring for you," Trevor barked.

"Dinner will be served in fifteen minutes, Miss Val." Henderson ignored Trevor Rogers.

"Thank you, Henderson. Will you ring the bell in the dining room to tell us?"

"Yes, miss."

"Her name is Mrs. Gilmartin," Trevor stated to the retreating Henderson. He whirled around to look at his cluster of children in front of the mantel. "Don't like that man, Val. Never will. Can't see how you keep him around. I told Binkie to fire him. Where is he by the way? We can't eat until he comes."

"Dinner will be served when the dining bell rings, Father," Val said mildly, bending down to spear a hot mushroom and ignoring his gimlet stare.

"Tell me about your baby, Carol . . . my godchild . . ." Val began.

"Not that you bothered to come out for the christening . . . you didn't," Trevor pointed out to no one in particular.

"Mary Valentina is beautiful, and she has dark curly hair, and brown eyes . . ." Carol gushed, smiling at her husband, who watched her fondly.

76

Val wondered how her father could not see that his progeny were very much in love with their spouses. How like Father not to see anything that would not be quite de rigueur in his circle. Love. What a misplaced waste of time and energy.

There were scuffling noises at the door, then Binkie burst into the lounge, red-faced and flustered. "Sorry I'm late. Fender bender. Damn fool said it was my fault. I called the police."

"Did they arrest you, Binkie?" Carol asked, giggling, earning glares from her target and her father.

"They gave me a ticket . . . yes." Binkie poured himself a martini, ignoring the jibes. "Trevor . . . how are you . . . been meaning to call you about the Landers contract."

"I have all the information. . . ." Trevor stated. "Going to put the squeeze on him tomorrow." He sipped his sherry with great relish.

When the dining bell rang, Trevor was inclined to hold back, but since Binkie promptly got to his feet from his seat in front of the hot mushroom canapes and strode from the room, he reluctantly followed.

Dinner was plain, but the tuna steaks were succulent, broiled in lemon and drawn butter with a soupçon of fresh-grated black pepper and fresh dill. The spinach was crisp and topped with large sliced mushrooms and crumbled blue cheese. The dressing was Henderson's own, and no one but he knew the recipe.

"I like potatoes lyonnaise with tuna," Trevor stated as Henderson cleared the plates.

"Really, sir? I think they serve it that way down on the wharf. Had you told me, I could have driven you down there." He swung through the door, not looking at Val as she coughed and swallowed water from her glass.

Binkie stared openmouthed at the swinging door leading into the kitchen as though he didn't believe what had just transpired.

Carol and Ruth were both hiding behind their napkins. Les and Michael made no attempt to hide their mirth.

Trevor glared at them. "Must you be as unseemly as that servant?"

Val stared down the table at her father. "Trevor"—she had been taught to call him that as a child, but she had always called him "Father" unless they argued—"Henderson is not a servant. He is the custodian of this house . . . and my friend . . ."

"This is Binkie's house." Trevor pushed out his chin.

"Not after this evening . . ." Val crossed her fingers under the table. "He's brought papers with him tonight that I will sign that will make me the owner of the House on Lombard Street."

Binkie nodded slowly when Trevor's head swiveled to him, like a bull on the charge. "That's right. She insists I sell it to her." He shrugged. "Besides, I never liked the house . . . nor do I trust . . ." Binkie paused as Henderson came into the room carrying a tray with the sliced Neopolitan bombe on plates. He left the room after serving the dessert and pouring more coffee.

". . . Henderson." Binkie finished before spooning some of the bombe into his mouth and closing his eyes in enjoyment.

"I'll pay you double what she's giving you." Trevor saw that he had the attention of everyone at the table, smiled, and began eating his dessert.

Val saw Michael's face redden, Les's mouth grow tight, as she stared at Binkie until he looked at her. His mouth opened and closed like a netted trout.

"Ah . . . Trevor . . . I have given Val my word that she could have the house. I do not go back on my word." Binkie's face filled with dark blood as he stared at the man who had been his mentor since his high school days.

"Damn fool thing to do . . . give your word to Val on anything. You should know by now that she would hold you to something like that." Trevor glowered at him, then

78

turned the same low-browed scowl on his oldest child. "You were always trouble."

"So were you," Val said, then held her breath.

Trevor barked a laugh. "You remind me too damn much of your mother."

Val placed her napkin next to her plate in the precise way she had been taught at the Villeneuve Finishing School, hoping that no one had noticed the tremor in her hand, nor the queasiness she was trying to mask behind her hand.

# CHAPTER FIVE

It gratified Val when Michael called her and told her that they would be flying down the next Thursday to have dinner with her and that Carol had told him she would bring Mary Val to see her godmother.

She and Henderson continued to take their walks to the club every morning and swim, and though her queasiness was still with her, prompt action with the tea and dry toast seemed to keep it in check.

As they were striding along one morning back to the house for breakfast, Henderson stopped, staring across the street. Val followed his glance, seeing a dog lying limp at the other side of the street near the curb.

"Is it dead?" Val asked him.

He didn't answer, just crossed the narrow street, touched the animal, then picked it up into his arms, carrying it to their block. Val trotted alongside Henderson as he strode to the house.

"No tags, still breathing," Henderson said laconically as he examined the dog on the kitchen floor. "It seems pretty weak. I'll take it to the veterinarian down the hill after I drop you at work."

"We'll take him to the vet first," Val called back to him as she hurried up the back stairs and went to her room to dress.

The veterinarian told them to leave the dog and that he would have an answer for Henderson when he returned from taking her to work. The animal hospital had a staff,

80

and the woman vet who took the dog seemed very gentle to Val.

"Will you call me at work and let me know?" Val asked him before she stepped to the pavement in front of the Twin Towers.

Henderson nodded, waited until she was in the building, then drove away.

The show went smoothly, and Dean was congratulating her and himself when Jane waved to her. "Call on line two, Mrs. Gilmartin."

"Hello, Val Gilmartin speaking."

"Hello, Val. This is Emma Cravick speaking. Dan's mother. How are you?"

Val held the phone in front of her staring into it, paralyzed.

"Hello? Val, are you there?"

"Ah . . . hello . . . yes, I'm here, Mrs. Cravick. How are you?"

"Fine. I am sorry it has taken us this long to talk to one another. It would be so nice to get together . . . to talk . . . have dinner . . . wouldn't it?"

"Huh? Oh . . . yes . . . so nice." Val coughed to try and clear the squeak from her voice.

"Lovely. We'll do it tonight. Is there any special place you prefer?"

"Me? I was going to eat at home."

"We'd love to join you. How kind of you to ask us."

"Us?" Val croaked.

"Yes. My brothers-in-law will be joining us, Yanos and Petros. I'm sure Dan has mentioned them to you."

"Yes . . . he has. Mrs. Cravick . . . about tonight . . ."

"My dear, do call me Emma. My name is English, and of course my parents were born there, so my name will be easy for you to remember."

"Nice." Val tried to rally.

"What address are you?"

81

"Lombard Street . . ." Val gulped air, gave the number and the directions.

"Stavros will find it."

"Stavros?" Val quizzed in a whisper, wondering if this was another uncle.

"He accompanies us everywhere . . . driver . . . body-guard . . ." Emma Cravick sang through the phone.

"Why do you need a bodyguard?" Val wondered if Dan's family was tied in with crime.

"Dan fusses when his uncles aren't with me . . . so Stavros is my constant companion. Good-bye, dear."

"Beats having a German shepherd . . ." Val moaned into the now dead phone. God. Dan's family coming to dinner . . . Henderson.

Val dialed the house with shaking fingers. No answer. She tried again. She buzzed Jane to keep trying her home phone number.

Finally Jane was able to get Henderson at home.

"The dog is a mutt, Miss Val, but a nice dog. He must have gotten free of his pen. No tags . . . nothing, so the doctor gave him a series of shots. He's old enough not to be a baby, but he's still a young dog . . ." Henderson was waxing enthusiastic about the dog. Several times Val tried to interrupt, but she wasn't able. "The vet says according to the chart of dogs he has that this one has Great Pyrenees in it . . . and maybe some retriever . . ."

"Henderson . . ." Val squalled. "Dan's . . . family . . . his mother . . . called. She and his uncles are coming to dinner. What will we do?"

"Serve bouillabaisse . . . and an endive salad with Anjou pears. Cheese and fruit for dessert. Turkish coffee . . . maybe . . ."

"Make it Greek." Val gulped. "I'll try to get out early . . . don't bother coming for me. I'll grab a cab."

"Don't take the cable car," Henderson admonished her, not hanging up the phone until she promised.

Val couldn't concentrate on anything for the rest of the

day. What did his mother want? Why was she coming to the house? What was she doing in California? Why were his uncles here? She put her hand on her rounding abdomen. They mustn't know about the baby. They would be possessive. They would want it. Val put her other hand over her stomach as well. This was her baby.

Dan loomed big in her mind. She wanted him near her. Why had she ever left New York? Why had she ever left him? She would have to beg him to take her back now. She shook her head slowly. She couldn't do that. Why? If that is all of life you have left, then why not beg for it?

Val put her head in her hands, remembering. Was Dan right? She didn't give enough credit to him and what he did. Football was his life . . . a life chosen by him, that had been good to him. Was she a snob about his life? "No," Val answered out loud. "I'm not that. Maybe I'm just a little bit jealous of something that he loves so much . . ."

Val sat back in her office chair stunned by what she had just spoken out loud. Jealous? Of football? She pushed her face into her hands. Why did I have to love him? Why does he mean so much to me?

She caught a cab that evening feeling as though she had carried the Golden Gate Bridge on her back all day. She snoozed in the cab, coming to herself and paying the man in a groggy fashion when she alighted in front of her house. Her house! Yes, it was that now, and it had taken a good share of saved money to come up with the down payment. The monthly payments would be good-sized too, Val thought, dragging up the steps to the front door that was opened before she could insert her key.

"You're exhausted. That's not good for the baby," Henderson told her. "You have time for a nap and a shower before the guests arrive. I'll bring up some tea."

Val nodded, not turning around as she mounted the stairs to her room. She kicked off her shoes before she flopped down on the bed. She was asleep in minutes. Dan was there moments after, in her head, but so real. She could feel him take her in his arms, undress her, love her as he so often did. Nothing could keep her from him. She lifted her arms and caught him to her.

The buzzer didn't penetrate her dream of Dan at first. In fact, even as she wakened she was sure that Dan was lying beside her. " 'Lo. Ah . . . oh . . . yes, Henderson . . . I'm getting up."

Sluggish and disoriented, Val swung her legs to the floor, feeling the immediate upheaval of her insides. She saw the teapot sitting on the silver tray on the dresser, went to it like a drowning man to a lifeline, and sipped the hot brew.

The phone rang as she put down the cup and was heading for the bathroom. She frowned at it. Why would Henderson put a call through when he knew that she would have to hurry as it was.

"Hello."

"Val? Dan. Listen, my mother and uncles—"

"Are coming here to dinner this evening . . . and if I don't hurry, they'll be here before—"

"What? They're coming there. Jeeez-zus. Val, I didn't tell them to get in touch with you. . . ."

"I didn't think you did." Val reveled in that voice. She wanted to scream at him that she didn't want his mother and uncles there; she wanted him beside her.

"Listen . . . Val . . . my uncle Yanos . . . don't pay any attention to him. He says anything that comes to his mind. . . ." Dan sounded agitated. "He's my uncle and I love him . . . but he can sometimes be very . . . gruff . . . outspoken . . . Damn, I wish I was there . . ."

You don't wish it any more than I do, Val thought, biting her lip and trying not to scream into the phone to Dan to come and get her.

"Ah . . . Val . . . my mother and uncles are going to stay in California for the exhibition game with the Forty-Ni-

84

ners. Would you like to come to the game?" Dan had seemed to stop breathing.

"Yes . . . yes, I would." I'd crawl all the way to Malibu Beach to see you fill a sand pail, Val whimpered in her mind.

"I'd like to see that house on Lombard that Binkie owns where you're staying. . . ." Dan said, some of his old rashness back in his tone.

"I bought it from Binkie. You should see it." Val was beaming into the phone, anxious to show Dan her purchase.

"You bought it?" There was a long silence. "I guess that means you're not coming back to New York . . ." Dan exhaled a deep breath into the phone. "I wish you luck with it, Val. I'll send the tickets for the game."

"Don't hang up . . . don't hang up . . ." Val said into the dead phone. "It doesn't mean that I'm not coming back to New York." She swiped at the sudden tear that trickled down her cheek. "Pregnant women cry a lot." She sniffled as she stepped into the shower.

She had a time choosing her dress, finally settling on a kaftan of silky cotton turquoise, gold low-heeled slippers of softest kid on her feet, no stockings. Panty hose had begun to be uncomfortable and she didn't want the constricted feeling to make her any more tense on top of everything else. Her left hand rubbed the skin of her abdomen. It itched with what Dr. Cross called stretch marks.

"Sometimes it happens like that, Val. Many times, slender, narrow-hipped women pop out in front, and their concave skin and tissue complain . . . thus stretch marks that itch and burn at times. That's why I'm giving you this ointment. It should help it."

Val pulled in her kaftan and looked at herself. "You're getting a basketball, that's what's in there . . ." She turned at the scuffling at the partially open door, and the dog, all bandaged around the middle with one paw wrapped and taped gauze on the top of his head, skidded around the

85

opening, then paused to look at her with his tongue hanging out the side of his mouth. "You look like World War Three, but you seem frisky enough." Val spoke mildly, not having really been introduced to the creature, who now, cleaned up, looked like a rather broad-bodied golden retriever.

He ambled forward, his body quivering inside the loose casing of his skin. He sat down and lifted his paw to Val.

"Oh, good dog . . ." Val crooned, cradling the basketlike head. "You're so sweet. I'm sorry we have to run an ad to find your owners. It would be nice if you could stay here." Val patted his head and rose to her feet. "I can't believe it. When I was a kid, all I ever wanted was a dog . . . now I have a dog, maybe, and a cat. What was it Mrs. Hernandes called a dog? *Per . . . perro.* That's it. I'll call you Perro. Boy dog." She waggled her finger at the wriggling animal sitting at her feet. "I'll bet Henderson doesn't know you're up here. Come along with me. I'll take you down the back stairs. . . ." Val sighed. "Then I have to face my guests . . . or the firing squad . . . whichever comes first." She stared down gloomily at the dog, then urged him down the back staircase. She watched him clatter down some steps, then retraced her own down the hall to the front stairs. "Dan's mother won't like me. She's come to California to tell me to stay out of Dan's life. I'm too old for him. She wants grandchildren . . . but not mine. I know . . ." Val heaved another shuddering sigh and descended the stairs as though she were going to the guillotine.

She pushed open the doors to the lounge. "I'm Valen—" A quivering, wagging, clumsy, golden package pushed past her into the room charging at the inhabitants as Val watched in horror. "Perro . . . stop . . . don't . . . heel . . ." Goggle-eyed, Val watched him place his face into Henderson's special vegetable dip, then lift it, looking like he had a Santa Claus beard.

"Damn him. How did he get in here, Miss Val?" Henderson pushed around the frozen Val into the melee in front of the fireplace.

"He is a big one that . . . young, too." A black-mustachioed man with silver streaks in his black mane of hair took hold of the golden-coated dog and held him against his blocky frame.

"He must have followed me down the stairs," Val ventured huskily, her eyes going to the woman with the light brown hair streaked with white, her hairstyle the height of fashion, the silk dress in beige simple yet elegant. All at once she grinned, and Val felt light-headed. It was Dan's grin.

In minutes, Henderson had the dog in control and out of the room. He was back again in minutes to take Yanos's jacket and assure him that there would be no mark after he cleaned it. At the same time he left a tray of hot canapes on the table, whisked off the offending dip, and disappeared.

"I was not worried about the jacket . . . and you must not be, little lady who is chewing her bottom lip. . . ." Yanos came over to her and nearly lifted her from her feet in a hug. "I am Uncle Yanos and you are Valentina."

"Yes," Val squeaked. Why did all the finishing school training desert her now?

"Yanos, put her down. Come here, my dear, and let me look at you." Emma Cravick took Val's hand in hers and looked at her for long moments. "Yes . . . you are every bit as beautiful as Dan said you were. Is she not, Petros?"

"Yes . . . beautiful." A less hulking man came forward, no less dark but with a lighter mustache and a very sweet smile. He kissed Val on both cheeks and then stood back to look at her as well. "So, you have a dog too. Danilo told us of the cat . . . we did not know about the dog."

"He just arrived. Henderson and I found him. He was hurt. We took him to the vet." Val blushed at her babbling, then stood there squeezing her hands in front of her, looking at the three people who stared back at her. When

87

they smiled, she gave an audible sigh of relief, making Yanos laugh.

"So . . . you thought we would eat you, eh?" He nodded his head like a black bear would. "Did not Danilo warn you that I would not chew you up?" He laughed at his own joke.

Val felt herself relaxing, her indigestion fading somewhat. "He told me not to mind anything you said." Val smiled as she took the seat next to Dan's mother.

"The puppy." Yanos roared, "I will smack him."

"Not anymore you won't, brother. He is liable to pick you up and throw you through the window."

"Oh . . . no . . . Dan would never do that. He's too gentle," Val said, then leaned forward to take a hot chestnut from the chafing dish. She looked up at the silence and saw three persons staring at her in wonderment. "What's wrong?"

"Danilo was considered a terror as a boy . . . temper . . . strength . . . unruliness. It made him a fine football player . . . but he was often in trouble," Petros pointed out mildly, paying no attention to the angry grunts of his brother.

"Danilo only lost his temper when he should," Yanos stated, his brows coming together over his nose.

"Dear Yanos, you defend my bad boy . . . but Petros was right. He could be very hard to handle at times . . . even I thought so, and he was always gentle with me." Emma Cravick speared one of the chestnuts with a tiny silver fork. "Ummm, these are good, dear. You must tell me how to make them."

"Yes, I will." Val led the way to the dining room after a short interval, fast becoming not only intrigued with Dan's family but also relaxed and pleased with their friendliness.

The bouillabaisse made a hit.

"The food is good. This Henderson is one smart fellow with the bread," Yanos pronounced, shaking his head like a bear while holding a roll in his hand. All at once he speared Val with those black-brown eyes of his. "I will tell you a story, Valentina. Once I was much in love with my Eleni. I told her to wait for me in Greece while I made my fortune in America. She begged to come with me . . . but I was too ashamed of being poor. I wanted the best of things for her. She only wanted to marry me. I was in this country five years when her father made her marry another. She had three children that should have been mine. When she was a widow and sick, her three children gone to Australia to live, I went to get my Eleni and bring her back to Pennsylvania. She had everything that a woman could want in a house for the three months that she lived there. I weep for her yet." The big man had not taken his eyes from Val. She could see a sheen of tears in his gaze. "I tell you, Valentina, that pride squeezes love, flaws it, cuts it, and leaves it to die. . . ." He coughed. "I should have taken my Eleni with me and not let anything stand in the way. I live with that . . ." He put his napkin at the side of his plate.

Val took in deep breaths, feeling the pain of Yanos, feeling his tears on her own cheeks. She put a shaking hand to her mouth. She cleared her throat. "Thank you for telling me such a beautiful story . . ."

He leaned forward, pushing his plate back on the table. "Learn from this, young lady. Do not let pride spoil your life."

Openmouthed, Val looked from one to the other. Dan's mother was watching her, a gentle smile on her face. Petros was nodding slowly, his lips upturned at the corners. "Ah . . . but . . . you see . . . Dan wants his freedom. . . ." Val felt as though she had just told a lie. She didn't believe what she had just said. She had verbalized her fear and given it out as Dan's thoughts. "What I mean is . . . Dan is in a very exciting career. He meets many . . . people . . . women . . ."

"All men meet women wherever they go, child," Emma

Cravick stated, her voice a little tart as though she were impatient with Val. "My Danilo, Dan's father, was a very handsome man . . . women were always attracted to him. . . ." She paused and looked at her brothers-in-law when they laughed. "Yes . . . you knew about it . . . you saw how the women chased him . . . but Danilo loved me. It was *me* he chased . . . it was my father he defied when he married me. I always knew that he loved me . . . and loves me still. . . ." Emma Cravick smiled serenely.

Val looked at Petros as though he too must have a story to tell her, but he just smiled and nodded. "I wanted a career too," Val tried to explain.

"Does Danilo say no to this?" the mild Petros asked.

"No . . . of course not . . . but . . ."

"Then I see no problem here," Yanos bellowed, then surged to his feet. "I like to have my dessert in the front room as we do at home." He left the dining room like a bull on the charge, Val's mouth still hanging open as she watched him.

Emma Cravick patted her hand. "Don't worry, dear. Yanos approves of you . . . and he certainly never took to many people as fast. Wouldn't you agree, Petros?"

"Yes." The soft-spoken Greek helped both women from their chairs and followed the hurricane named Yanos. "My dear, I hope you do not mind . . . but Stavros was so anxious to meet you that I told my sister-in-law's driver that he might come into the lounge to meet you." Petros seemed to inhale deeply after saying so many words.

"I don't mind," Val responded, wondering at what point she had lost control of the situation. It was up to her to point out to the Cravicks that she and Dan were no longer together . . . but she hadn't the courage to do so. If they had disliked her, it would have been much easier . . . but somehow they didn't disapprove of her. Val shook her head, confused, and smiled at Uncle Petros when he held the door of the lounge for her as she followed Dan's mother.

Stavros came into the room holding Perro on a rope lead. "I have brought the dog with me . . . to show you that he will be easy to train."

Val gaped at him.

"Stavros is very good with animals and children," Emma Cravick informed her, patting her hand.

"That so?" Val was floundering.

"You are a fool," Yanos bellowed. "You must have a paper for him."

"No," Stavros shouted back, a bemused Henderson following behind with the coffee cart and the cheese and fruit. "I use my voice."

"Pah . . . foolishness," Yanos riposted at earsplitting range.

"They are very fond of one another . . . truly," Dan's mother said placidly, gesturing to Henderson that she would pour the coffee.

"Wonderful," Val whispered, fascinated, feeling warmed by this crazy family. She gave Henderson a lop-sided smile when he looked flabbergasted as he left the room to answer the phone.

When he returned, Stavros had Val on her feet, showing her how she must train the dog. Perro was delighted to be part of the circus of humans. Yanos had screwed up the evening paper and was shoving that into Val's hand. Petros was sipping coffee; his sister-in-law was biting daintily into a piece of Brie.

"Miss Val . . . telephone . . ." Henderson coughed to gain her attention.

Val looked up, flustered. "Tell them to call later."

"It's . . . Mr. Cravick."

"If it is Danilo . . . bring the phone in here. I will speak to him," Yanos pronounced in his basso profundo.

Val was too busy with the dog and Stavros to object, but when she heard Yanos on the phone, she cringed.

"What do you mean . . . have I bullied her? Of course not. Stavros and I are teaching her how to train the dog.

91

What dog? Her dog, of course, the one she calls Perro. Well, it is not my fault that you do not know what your wife is doing. . . ."

"Aaaaaagh . . ." Val swung around as she heard this, her eyes fixed on the phone, then swinging to look at Petros and Dan's mother. Dan's mother was now sedately eating a grape. Petros was still sipping his black-as-death coffee.

"Stop shouting, Danilo. It is bad for your throat. What are you saying? You sound like a madman. No, of course we are not training the dog in the dining room. He is with us in the lounge. I need to have my coffee . . . if your mother will pour it . . ." Yanos glared at his sister-in-law, who calmly handed him a cup. ". . . Why should I take the dog outside? You do not mind, do you, Valentina?"

"Ah . . . me? No . . . I don't mind." And she didn't. What she minded was Yanos referring to her as Dan's wife. Surely they knew it wasn't true. It was a slip of the tongue, she was sure. Val turned back to Stavros.

"He wants to speak to you, Emma." Yanos held the phone toward his sister-in-law. "I think he is drinking. He keeps swearing."

Emma Cravick frowned as she took the phone. "I hope you were not swearing at your uncle, Dan. I wouldn't like that. Dear, you're shouting. Surely I've taught you better. What? The dinner? Very good. Why would you think anything was wrong? That's silly. We're having a delightful time. Would you like to speak to your uncle Petros?" Without waiting for a reply she handed the phone to her quiet brother-in-law.

"Hello, Danilo? What? No, of course there is no trouble here." He twinkled at Val as she marched around the room with the dog, Henderson and Stavros watching her. She watched the phone.

"Here you are, my dear. Danilo wishes to speak with you." Petros handed her the phone and took the leashed dog from her. "Here, Stavros, let me show you how you should hold the leash."

"You . . . show us . . ." bellowed Yanos.

Stavros glared at both of them. Henderson watched closely. Emma Cravick poured more coffee.

Val walked the length of the long cord of the phone to the opposite side of the room before speaking into it. "Hello."

"God . . . Val . . . it sounds awful . . . what a din." Dan groaned.

"Pandemonium . . . actually." Val couldn't keep back a laugh as the voices across the room rose a decibel.

"Bloody awful . . . that's what it is . . . listen to me, Val . . . I . . . I didn't know my mother would call you . . ." He stammered, surprising Val, making her feel powerful . . . more powerful than a linebacker.

"Ashamed of me?" Val prodded him.

"Damn you . . . don't make fun of me . . . my family . . ."

". . . are teaching me how to train the dog . . ."

"What the hell is going on with you anyway? First a cat . . . now a dog. You've never had animals."

Val inhaled. "I have discovered new things about myself . . . one is that I always wanted a dog. . . . Cats I didn't care for, but you have to admit that Gato has personality."

"He's a ham." Dan chuckled, telling her an anecdote about the cat.

"You're still at the brownstone." The thought made her feel warm all at once. She patted her tummy with her free hand.

"Ah . . . yes . . . remember I said that I wouldn't leave until . . ."

"Yes, I remember. You should stay there . . . so that Gato won't be lonely."

"Right."

"Dan, your uncle said something . . ." Val was going to mention that Yanos had referred to her as Dan's wife.

"Dear, might I speak to my son?" Emma stood at Val's elbow, smiling, holding out her hand for the phone.

"Of course." Val stepped back without saying anything else to Dan, though she could hear him calling her name.

"Dan, dear, I can't tell you how we've enjoyed meeting Val . . . and we feel lucky to have found her free one evening so that we could dine together. How like you to choose such a popular lady. Good-bye, dear. Don't catch cold."

Val stared at Dan's mother as she glided back to her place on the settee and poured herself just a bit more coffee.

"Do come and sit down, Val. This coffee is quite good." Not waiting to see if Val sat, she looked around at the dog. "I do believe he is coming along, Stavros. Since we shall be staying in the area for a time, I think you should come over every day and help with the dog."

Stavros nodded once.

Val sensed that even if she didn't want the taciturn chauffeur around it wouldn't matter. Emma Cravick was the boss. Val felt herself sinking into a marshmallow sea. She had to explain to the Cravicks that, not only was she not Dan's wife, she was no longer his live-in lover, either.

The evening wound down without a word coming out of her mouth to that effect. Instead she promised them that she would come to their hotel, the Hyatt Regency, for dinner with them.

"And tomorrow, my dear, Stavros will fetch you, and you and I shall indulge in the dim sum, that lovely blending of luncheon and afternoon tea that the Chinese are famous for. Our lawyers, Hathaway and Finn, have told me that Ling's is one of the best . . ."

Val was still opening her mouth trying to tell Mrs. Cravick that she wouldn't be able to make lunch, that she had a meeting that might run through lunch, when the Cravick family went down the front steps and into the car that Stavros had brought round for them.

Val wandered back into the lounge as Henderson locked the front door, surprised to find Perro at her side, pressing his muzzle into her hand.

"Sorry, Miss Rogers. I must not have shut the door properly."

"That's fine." Val rubbed the silky, strong-boned head. "He is a very good looking mutt, wouldn't you say, Henderson?"

"Yes, miss, I would say that. He also has a good disposition. Not once did he try to snap at all the people around him tonight . . . and it wasn't a quiet group," Henderson finished dryly, making Val laugh.

"Aren't they the loveliest people? It's like getting a shot of sunshine to have the Cravicks around, isn't it?"

"Yes, miss, just what you've always needed." Henderson took the dog by the collar and urged him through into the kitchen before Val could ask him what he meant.

Yawning, she shrugged. She had to get to bed. She could talk to him in the morning.

The next day, Val had to excuse herself near the end of her meeting, saying that she had a luncheon appointment. Brewer looked at her, then nodded.

"I know how it is to have a business luncheon." Brewer frowned, then looked back at the papers in front of him.

Val felt a little guilty about not telling Brewer it was not a business meeting, yet she had absolutely no idea how she would have described Dan's mother to him.

Stavros was waiting in the car. Without a word he whisked her through the traffic winding down streets that in New York would have been called alleys. When he stopped in front of a place with the sign Ling's on the window, Val privately thought it looked more like a tailor shop than a restaurant.

"My dear, here I am . . ." Emma hailed her from a small booth along the wall. "Isn't this quaint? Val, my dear, you look smashing in that purple dress. Cotton, isn't it? Why don't you take off the jacket?"

95

"No need. I'm a bit chilly." Val knew that her rounded tummy showed a bit when her jacket was removed.

"Really? It's so lovely and warm today." Emma looked at her for a long moment. "But then . . . the jacket looks so nice."

Dim sum was a revelation to Val. She had heard of it being served in the Chinese restaurants in New York, but she had never tried it. The variety of filled pastries, meat, fish, and vegetable was pleasing and piquant to her palate, and though she had found that if she ate too much she had the inevitable heartburn, she was unable to resist the succulent delicacies. She even had a sweet pastry with her fragrant tea.

Both she and Emma pronounced the culinary adventure of dim sum to be a rousing success.

During the afternoon Val was sorry she had indulged herself. By late afternoon she had a headache and indigestion.

By the time Henderson picked her up after work, she had a real tummy upset.

"Not to worry, Miss Val. I have a remedy that might help. On my mother's side I have Nez Perce Indian blood. I have a few herb recipes."

Val shook her head, not opening her eyes until they reached home. She went up the stairs holding her head, quite sure that she would have to cancel her dinner with Dan's family.

After drinking the herbal tea that Henderson had made, she slept, waking to a feeling of well-being and relaxation.

She donned a rose silk suit, leaving the top button at the waist of the skirt undone, the Chanel jacket a good disguise for her rounding form. "Soon you'll have to get into maternity clothes, fatso," she told her mirror image, patting the baby. "What will Dean and old Curtis say about this, I wonder." She shrugged. "I don't care what they say. My baby is important to *me*. Other opinions don't matter."

She donned her wine kid slings with matching bag with the gold chain shoulder strap, checked to see that her pink sapphire earrings and pin were secure, patted her platinum hair coiled in a French twist, and went down the stairs whistling.

Henderson was waiting in the foyer to drive her to the Embarcadero Plaza. "Remedy worked."

"Like a charm." Val smiled at him.

The evening was crisp but warm, fresh but not damp when she alighted from the car and told Henderson that she would call him to tell him what time to fetch her.

She took the elevator to the suite high above the city. Since there were only three doors in the thickly carpeted corridor, it was no trouble to find the right one and ring the buzzer.

When the door opened, Val almost fainted.

"Hello, Val." Dan put his hand under her elbow and led her into the apartment.

# CHAPTER SIX

Val looked at the Cravick family blankly, seeing their lips move but not comprehending. She took the drink that Yanos pressed into her hand and gulped it, not realizing the clear liquid was gin until it hit her throat and environs. Her eyes watered with the effort not to cough. She coughed anyway.

"Uncle Yanos . . ." Dan growled. "Val doesn't drink. Just a little wine now and then . . ." He put his arm around her, taking the drink from her hand.

"Of course she drinks. She just finished that very dry martini. Would you like another, Valentina?" Yanos smiled at her, handing her a cocktail napkin so that she could wipe her eyes and nose.

"No thank you . . ." Val gasped. "One's my limit."

Petros came forward with a taller glass of clear liquid. He laughed when Val eyed it warily. "Not to worry, Miss Rogers . . . this is seltzer water."

"Her name is Gilmartin . . . Mrs. Gilmartin." Dan spoke somewhat stiffly, his arm still around Val's waist as they faced his family.

His mother came forward, taking Val's outstretched hand. "Val dear, didn't we have a lovely time today?" Not waiting for a reply, Emma turned to look at her son, her one eyebrow arching. "Are you not going to release her for the rest of the evening?"

Val felt Dan's hand clench at her waist.

"I may not." Dan's chin jutted forward, making Val

stare up at him. What had made him lose his temper? And he was furious, Val could tell.

She had moved toward the lounge, following his uncles and his mother, when Dan's arm tightened on her and he leaned down to whisper to her.

"Who the hell have you been dating? And who is this Henderson that lives with you now?"

"Do you have a slice missing in your loaf?" Val hissed at him. "I've told you about Henderson hundreds of times."

"My mother says he waits on you hand and foot." Dan's chiseled features had a steely menace.

She felt her mouth sag open. "He's the custodian of the house. He has been for years."

"What about the other men you've dated since you've been out here? My mother says you're never home."

Val looked from him through the arched doorway leading to the lounge at the placid woman sitting in front of a coffee table. "I don't know . . . you must have misunderstood your mother. She said you were hard to handle," Val finished petulantly and illogically. She pulled free of him and stalked into the lounge.

"There you are, dear. How nice." Emma smiled at Val just as the door buzzer sounded again. "Ah . . . that must be your family. Petros, will you get that?"

"My what?" Val whispered, her mouth gone flaccid.

"Your family, Valentina." Emma sounded out each word as she gestured Val to sit opposite her.

"I prefer to stand," Val said woodenly, turning toward the door as though she had just been chosen to be greeter at a witch doctor's convention. God, her father was shaking hands with Petros . . . there was Carol . . . and Les . . . and the baby . . . and Michael . . . and . . .

"What the hell is going on, Mother?" Val heard Dan's savage whisper. "Why are these people here?" He approached Val and put his arm around her again. "This is upsetting to Val. Mother . . ."

99

"Dan . . . never mind . . ." Val squeaked, her hands plucking at the sleeve of his suit.

Emma Cravick rose to her feet and glided forward to greet her guests, her sunny smile a direct contrast to Trevor Rogers's glower.

"Do come in," Emma said, reaching for the baby, then turning to look at Val. "Your niece is so lovely, Valentina."

"Yes, she is, isn't she." Val moved forward, feeling Dan stay at her side, her growling stomach forgotten as she watched Mary Val coo at Dan's mother. "This is what we wanted, isn't it, Yanos?" Emma sighed, then looked at Val sadly.

"Mother . . . what the hell . . ." Dan began his voice on a normal tone, his anger building.

"Ooooh, look, Dan, she wants you to hold her." Mrs. Cravick thrust the drooling baby into the huge quarterback arms, smiling serenely when her son gulped and froze in place.

Val watched him with Mary Val, seeing that rock-hewn face soften as the baby gurgled at him. She felt the sting of tears as Dan held the baby a little closer, his smile widening.

"Isn't she cute, Val?" Dan didn't take his eyes off the baby as he spoke.

"Yes, she is. She's my godchild."

"Is she?" Dan grinned at her. "Lucky you. I don't have anything like this."

"Have your own," Yanos shouted, making the baby blink, Trevor wince, and Carol giggle.

When Yanos took hold of Trevor's hand, Val had a bad moment, wondering if her father would make some scathing remark to the bluff Greek.

Ruth came forward and lifted the baby from Dan's arms. "Aunts have rights too, you know." Her soft-spoken words accompanied by a smile found a response in Dan.

100

"I'm Ruth Rogers, Michael's wife." She jiggled the baby on her hip.

"I'm Dan . . ."

"Oh, I know who you are. Everytime we talked on the phone to Val, she did nothing but talk of you. I feel I know you already," Ruth gushed.

Val looked at her sister-in-law, wondering if the shy, retiring person who had married her brother had taken up drinking.

"And I'm Carol, Val's sister. We're almost like family, aren't we?" Carol enthused, ignoring Val's sputtering protest. "Do come and meet my husband, Les. Ruth wants to hold the baby and talk to your mother."

"Yes. I do." Ruth walked away from Val, leaving her alone in the center of the lounge listening to the two women talk baby talk to the baby.

Val edged over to her brother, who was listening to Yanos and Petros talk to his father. "What is going on?" she gritted, standing behind him. "Tell me, Michael, what in hell is going on?"

"We came to dinner." Her brother turned to look at her, taking the cocktail that was handed to him and sipping some of it. He looked around him. "Nice suite."

"Michael, if you don't want me to kick you in the ankle . . . right this minute, then you tell me what this is all about." She flung her arm in a short arc to include the family.

He stared down at her. "Agitated, aren't you?"

"Yes. Now start talking."

"I like that rose silk on you. With your hair coiled like that, you look like a Nordic princess." Michael smiled at her.

"Michael . . . I'm counting to three . . ." Val inhaled.

"Didn't they teach you anything at . . ."

"One."

". . . that expensive school father . . ."

"Two."

"Really, Val . . . there's no need . . ."

"Three."

"Ow. Dammit, Val, that hurt." Michael hopped on one foot, splashing his drink.

Dan spun around in a crouch, snarling, bringing all talk to a halt. "What's wrong, darling?" He spoke the words through gritted teeth.

"Nothing . . . nothing . . ." Val went over to him, reaching up to touch the bronze-hard features, as she often did when Dan needed soothing. "I was just asking my brother something."

Dan stared down at her, his eyes going over her in slow assessment. "Your face is thinner. Are you tired? Are you overworking?" He seemed to forget the rest of the room, his arms going round her to pull her closer.

Val pressed her hands flat on his chest, determined not to let him hold her tight, sure that he would feel the difference in her body. "No . . . no, everything is fine."

"She just has such a busy social life. I really can't blame the men. Val is so attractive," Emma Cravick said sunnily, not seeming to notice the rush of dark blood up her son's neck, his teeth snapping together, his hands clenching and unclenching.

Trevor Rogers stared at the manifestation of an angry football player.

Carol took her baby from Ruth and murmured, "My goodness."

Les muttered, "Lord"

Michael swallowed his drink in one gulp and shook his head, his eyes going from Dan to Dan's mother.

Ruth said nothing.

Yanos and Petros laughed.

Val breathed a sigh of relief when a white-coated attendant entered the lounge of the suite and announced that dinner was served.

Emma rose and approached Trevor, taking his arm. "I

102

can't tell you how delighted the Cravick family is with dear Valentina."

"You act as though they were getting married." Trevor's eyes narrowed on the woman at his side, his words audible to those following.

"Wonderful. A wedding. I love weddings." Ruth cooed at the baby as she walked next to Carol. Her sister-in-law nodded her agreement.

"What has gotten into Ruth?" Val managed to say to Michael, who gave her a blank look.

Petros and Yanos stepped to either side of Val and each took an arm of hers. "My child, it is good to meet your family.' Yanos patted her arm with his skillet-sized hand. "Your father worries too much about the wrong thing . . . but the others I like."

"Thank you, sir." Michael was walking behind them with Dan. "I appreciate that. I would like to have lunch with you both one day."

Val could feel Dan's eyes on her without turning around.

"We would like that, wouldn't we, Petros? It is good to know the members of one's family."

Val staggered, feeling Petros's arm steadying her.

"Let me take her," Dan growled.

"My dear nephew, I think I can be trusted to help Val into her chair. Ah, here we are, let me help you." Petros eased her into the chair, then he and Yanos sat on either side of her, making their nephew glower.

"Uncle Petros, you can sit over there next to Carol." Dan gestured to an empty seat across the table.

"Thank you, Danilo. I'm quite comfortable." Petros smiled up at his nephew.

Dan then looked at Yanos, who shook his head and pointed across the table. Then he looked at his mother, his hands clenching and unclenching at his side.

"Dan, dear, do sit down so that we may begin," his mother said softly.

Dinner went well. Pâté was followed by broiled prawns in lime juice, saffron rice, and a marinated vegetable salad. The bread was a black rye, fresh baked and crusty.

Wine flowed with the food, and more than once Dan leaned across the table and told his uncle not to fill Val's glass.

"Don't be so dull, nephew," Yanos bellowed, making Carol laugh when the baby cooed from her carry cot near her mother. "She likes me," Yanos stated, brooking no argument. "Babies like me."

"I'm sure they do, Mr. Cravick." Ruth grinned at the bear of a man.

"You must call me Yanos. We are family now."

"What the hell does that mean?" Dan snarled, his head thrusting forward in menace.

"Do not swear in front of the women," Yanos bellowed, making Mary Val gurgle and Les and Michael chuckle behind their hands.

Dessert was crooned over by the women and appreciated by most of the men. Fresh-made éclairs. Neither Dan nor Val took any. Trevor was going to refuse but changed his mind.

After the meal Dan was at Val's side at once, ignoring the comments of his uncle Yanos who observed to the table in general that his nephew was acting like a puppy.

Dan nearly lifted her out of the dining room and down a hall to a bedroom. He shut the door behind them, then turned to stare at her. "How are you?"

Val looked at him, wanting him to kiss her and tell her that he missed her, that he needed her. "Fine. How are you?"

"Fine." Dan looked around the room. "I didn't know they invited your father . . . the whole family."

"I know that. *You* were as surprised as I was."

"More, I think. God, I hated it, meeting your father for the first time like that."

"He hasn't said much to you, has he?"

104

Dan shook his head. "He doesn't mask his feeling though. He doesn't see me as the man in your life."

"My father and I never agree on anything." Val felt breathless when she saw his first real smile of the evening.

When he approached her, she forgot to fend him off. It felt so good to be held in those strong arms again. She felt so safe.

"Hey . . . your face is thin, but you've put on weight in your middle." He grinned down at her. "Why are you blushing? You look wonderful. You've always been too slim, Val."

"Only a man who is around people two hundred pounds and over all the time would say that." Val managed a shaky smile. Tell him! Tell him now, the voice inside of her urged. "Dan . . ."

"Yes, honey." He was watching her, his blue eyes velvet soft.

The door crashed open. "They said that you would be kissing and that I should let you alone, but I said that you wouldn't mind when I told you what we are going to do." Yanos smiled at Val and ignored his scowling nephew.

"I should have locked the door," Dan muttered.

"If you want to be alone with your wife, take her home then. We are going with the family to the airport and have a drink before the plane leaves. Good-bye." Yanos crashed out the door again, leaving Val staring after him open-mouthed.

"There's no need for you to take me . . ." Val's voice trailed at the fury on his face.

"You're assuming that I'm not staying with you?" Dan spaced the words.

"Ah . . . I didn't think. I thought the team." She felt transfixed by those blue eyes.

"You thought wrong. I had my luggage delivered to your place. I came here from the airport because I would have been late and no doubt missed you at the house if I had tried to go there. I'm coming home with you, Val."

"Fine," she said, knowing she should argue, but feeling such a teary relief that he was coming with her she couldn't manage another word.

They walked out to the other room to find it empty, even the attendants gone.

"My mother should have waited to say good night to you." Dan shook his head. "I don't know what's gotten into her. She has never been like this."

"I think she's darling. We had such fun when we went out to lunch." Val described the dim sum to him as they took the elevator to the lobby and walked through the flower-festooned area. "Shall I call Henderson to come for us?" She felt light as air, as though she were floating. People passing by looked handsome, beautiful, an aureole of happiness around each one. She was afraid to open her mouth too wide lest she might begin singing. Perhaps she would play the piano when she returned to Lombard Street. She hadn't felt like touching the baby grand since she had come to California.

"No." Dan spoke at her ear, his body curving over hers as they walked. "I rented a car. You can give me directions."

"I'll give you a busman's tour on the way."

"Great."

Val had the feeling that neither of them was speaking their thoughts, but brick by brick, the wall that had been built between them by their separation was crumbling.

The car was a sleek, white Corvette.

"Were they out of Volkswagens?" Val chuckled.

"I think so." Dan reached over and grasped her knee. "Actually this car is an inconvenience. You could be over here sitting on my lap if it weren't for the gear shift." His hand stroked her knee. "Stockings feel nice." His voice slurred, making Val's heart lurch out of rhythm.

"Dangerous to drive one-handed," she squeaked.

"True." Dan left his hand on her leg, his fingers kneading the pliant, silk-covered flesh.

106

The drive down the Embarcadero was almost a total loss as far as Val was concerned. She stared out the window but saw nothing. Her only awareness was that Dan was here . . . with her . . . after such a long time apart.

They reached the house on Lombard Street, and still Val had been virtually silent. Val showed him the alleyway that would take them to the garage. "There's space for another car. . . ." Dan got out and punched the numbers Val had recited to him on the automatic door opener board.

When he turned off the car, went round to her side, opened the door, then pressed the automatic lock for the garage doors, they were cocooned in black silence.

Dan returned to her side, cursing once when he bumped into something.

"I'll get the light," Val offered.

"In a minute." Dan was back beside her, leaning down to her. Val could feel his breath on her face. "Val . . . don't ask me why I'm saying this in the dark . . . oh hell . . . Val, I think we should get married."

"What? Why?" She asked him, licking her dry lips.

"Ah . . . because it's a good idea . . . we're good together, Val. Listen, you don't have to give me your answer now. Just think about it tonight. We can talk tomorrow."

Val wanted to shake him. She didn't have to think about it. She wanted to fling herself into his arms. How could he be so cold and clinical about their life together? I should turn him down flat, she fumed, leading him to the small elevator that led to the kitchen or beyond to the second floor, knowing full well she wouldn't do that.

When she and Dan closed the door of the small lift, there was barely room.

"Ummmm, this is nice." He caught her close, his chin resting on the top of her head, his hands going over her as though in search of something. "I can't believe how round your tummy is. What have you been eating? Starches?"

107

"Pasta puts weight on, they say . . ." Val floundered.

"And you love pasta." Dan laughed, holding the door for her so that she could step from the tiny elevator.

Henderson stood there, a hammer clutched in his hand, his body crouched, Perro at his side growling. "Are you all right, Miss Rogers?" Despite the years he had on Dan, the fighter's body was alert and well muscled.

Dan took a deep breath, his eyes going from the dog to the rough-looking man, his hands hanging loose at his sides.

"Henderson! You scared me. It's all right. This is Dan Cravick, my . . . he . . ."

Henderson stepped forward, his hand outstretched. "I know who he is. 'Bout time you got here."

Perro, seeing the two men shake hands, went to Val in wriggling welcome, his golden furry head pressing into her hand.

"So this is the dog." Dan spoke behind her, bringing Perro's wary attention to him.

"This is Perro." Val smiled as Dan crouched in front of the dog, talking softly to it until the animal began rubbing against his hands. "He's pretty, isn't he, Dan?"

"Honey, this is a boy. He isn't pretty. He's handsome. Right fella?" Dan rose, still scratching the dog under the chin. "Which room is ours?" He looked around the up-stairs hall as Henderson pointed to the last door. He looked back at the retainer. "Thanks. Does the dog sleep downstairs?"

Henderson nodded, asked Val if she needed anything and was she all right, then he went down the stairs, the dog clattering after him.

Dan pushed open the door to their room. "Why did he ask you if you were all right? Have you been ill, Val?"

"Indigestion," Val told him truthfully.

"You? I don't believe it. Your stomach is almost as ironclad as mine."

"Do you want to shower or anything?" Val asked hurriedly.

"I'd like to . . . but I'd better get down and get my gear." Dan stared at her, eyes narrowed. "Is something wrong, Val? You're looking flustered again."

"Nothing is wrong. I've just decided I need a shower too. I'll use the one in the guest room." She grabbed at a dressing gown and turned to leave the room. She paused for a second. "And if I were you, I'd check the closets for my things. No doubt Henderson has unpacked your things already." She skipped out the door.

"Hey. What happened to the nice habit of showering together?" Dan's voice followed her down the hall.

"I'm not about to shower with someone who thinks I'm putting on weight." Her breath caught in her throat as he laughed. How she had missed that sound; how she had missed him.

She whisked off her clothes, looking at her naked body in the long mirror on the bathroom door. She was getting very round there. She had to tell Dan she was pregnant; she couldn't put it off.

She shampooed her hair, another excuse to give herself more time to think how to tell him. She sluiced off her hair and body then slathered her wet body with fragrant oil before drying it. The old-fashioned beauty secret had been the greatest safeguard of her delicate skin, keeping it soft and supple in any weather.

She dropped the wet towels down the laundry chute and was just about to don the dressing robe when the door to the bathroom was pushed open and Dan stood there, a brown toweling toga around his waist.

"I couldn't wait any longer. I've been without you too long, lady mine." He reached out for her, wrapped the dressing robe around her, and swept her up into his arms.

"I always forget how big you are." Val ran her hands over his bare shoulders.

"Do you? Well, you damn well won't forget anything

109

more about me. This is the last separation we have, Valentina."

Val felt her body go liquid as it was pressed against Dan. Had it been a hundred years since they had made love? No, it must have been two hundred. Smiling, she pressed her face into his neck, not releasing her hold on him as he placed her on the bed then joined her.

"What's so funny?" Dan ran his words together like poured honey, his eyes a blue fire as he pressed the wrap away from her body. "So, tell me the joke." His long fingers looked mahogany against the pinky whiteness of her skin.

"I was just thinking that it must have been two hundred years ago that we made love." Val's hands began the familiar exploration of his chest, her fingers plucking at the curling mat of black hair that arrowed down his body. "You are aroused, my man, are you not?"

"Damn right. I feel like my head is going to blow off." He bent his mouth toward her breasts, his lips closing around her nipple. "Ummmm, your breasts are even fuller. I never thought your breasts could get lovelier . . ." Dan's guttural assessment made her body flush with delight.

How was it that she only felt beautiful when she was with Dan? Why did her body come alive then? Her skin take on a special glow? Her eyes sparkle with gold fire? Her hair become more lustrous, thicker? "Dan . . . I wanted you with me." She sighed with relief. He was here. No more discomfort, no more indigestion, no more sleeplessness.

"Lord, lady mine, it was getting embarrassing. I'd start thinking about you when I was out on the field . . ." He groaned. ". . . I have never . . . I mean never . . . allowed anything to interfere with my concentration. I honestly thought nothing could."

"Is that when you were sacked? . . ."

"You saw the write-up," Dan said grimly, lying on his side, his face sliding over her body in intimate caress.

"Yes . . . I hated it. . . ." Val answered, her voice reedy.

Dan seemed to forget their conversation as he leaned up on one elbow to study her body. "You have skin like poured cream . . . your body, so tiny and curvy . . ." He muttered aloud, "I like your tummy and breasts . . ." His chuckle had a rasping sound to it. "I never thought you could be sweeter than you were . . . but you are. . . ." His lips caressed her abdomen, making her stomach muscles clench in delight. He slid down her body until his tongue was flicking over her instep.

Val's head turned and twisted on the pillow as remembered ecstasy filled her. No . . . not true, she thought, her mind churning with the emotion filling her. No memory could ever tell her how beautiful it was to be loved by Dan. Every nerve end quivered to life, her skin became thousands of sensors that flashed heat and joy to her inmost being. "Dan." She moaned. "Dan . . . don't leave me."

"Never. I'm with you until the end, my love. Tell me now you'll marry me. Tell me now."

"I will. I will marry you."

Dan moved up her body again until his mouth was centimeters from hers. "I, Danilo, take thee, Valentina . . . forever . . . even though that's not long enough."

"Daaaan." Val felt faint as his hands coursed over her, touching her with strong but gentle possession, taking her with his mouth and his body.

"I love your toenails. Pretty," Dan grunted, his mouth going over every inch of her again, even though Val's body was telegraphing to him that she was ready, that her body wanted to embrace him.

"Foolish man." Val pulled at his head, wanting him up close to her. "Dan . . . stop teasing me."

"No . . . I'm making love to you. I making up for all those nights of pacing the floor. . . ." Dan moved slowly, his hand making a sensual sweep up and down her body.

111

All at once his breathing was as ragged as Val's. He lifted her body with one arm, bringing her close to him, muttering love words into her skin. He positioned himself as he had always done with great care over her body, so that when he took her, at any time, she felt only him, not the weight of his large body.

"Dan . . . love me."

"I am. I will." His gentle plunge transfixed them both until the rhythm took them, spiraled them away.

After, when Val lay spent against his still-heaving chest, Dan cuddled her with his arms and body, pulling the sheet up around her. "So tiny . . . my baby so tiny." He kissed her, then took his arms from around her, edging away.

"Where are you going?" Val yawned.

"To get something. Be right back."

Val watched him go to the dressing room as her eyes fluttered closed.

"Hey, sleepyhead, open your eyes," Dan whispered, at her side again.

Val muttered, feeling her lips relax in a smile, "Go 'way." She wriggled closer to his warm body.

"Never. Open your eyes," Dan insisted, nuzzling her neck with his lips.

Yawning again, Val opened her eyes with an effort, focusing on a grinning Dan. He was holding something in his hand. Val blinked at the marquise-shaped diamond, gleaming pinkly in the light from the bedside lamp. Val looked at the ring, then at a laughing Dan, his face flushed. "Mine?"

"Yours." Dan picked up her left hand. "I should know your ring size by now . . . ahhh . . . a perfect fit. Do you like it?"

Val felt big globe-sized tears slipping down her cheeks into her ears. She gulped to stem the flood, but they only came faster.

"Honey, what is it? You never cry. Did I hurt you? Are

112

you sick?" Dan took hold of her chin, his fingers probing her neck and throat.

Fool, don't you know that pregnant women cry sometimes, Val thought in her watery mind, not able to verbalize her thoughts. "Love it." She babbled damply. "Lovely."

"Shall we fly to Las Vegas and get married? Now? Today?" Dan scooped her into his arms, cradling her to his large body.

"Can't." Val felt her face collapse. "Scrimmage game," she sobbed.

"Baby . . . shhhh . . ." Dan sounded alarmed.

Val was going to soothe him, tell him he was to be a father, but she decided instead to fall asleep. She woke once in the night, still enclosed in Dan's arms. She had a moment to wonder at her sense of well-being, then she was asleep again.

The next morning she woke and there was a note propped against the lamp on the side table telling her that Dan had left very early for a workout, that he would see her for dinner, hopefully.

She made it to the bathroom to be sick as usual, coming back to find the hot tea and dry toast sitting on the bedside table.

She dressed in her sweats and joined Henderson down in the foyer, Perro rising up from a rug to wag a welcome to her.

"Mr. Dan took Perro out for a run while it was still dark," Henderson informed her. "I hope this dog doesn't think that I will be getting up at the crack of dawn for him." Henderson gave the dog his fiercest scowl, getting a delighted yip in return.

They had walked more than halfway to the club when Val looked at the man beside her. "What do you think of my . . . of Dan?"

"I think he is the best medicine that you can have," Henderson pronounced.

"I . . . we . . . he asked me to marry him. I'm going to do it." She finished in a rush.

"Sensible." Henderson held open the door of the club. They nodded to a few acquaintances there, then each went their separate ways into the locker rooms.

As usual the swim after the brisk walk from the house had an energizing effect on Val.

When a woman a little older than herself came up to her after her shower, she looked up with a smile.

"I just had to say something when I saw you were pregnant. I'm Elaine Vogt and I've had three children. Is this your first?"

Val's hand went to her abdomen. If this woman could tell she was pregnant, why couldn't Dan? Was he fooling her? "Yes."

"Well . . ." The short woman shrugged. "In this day and age when no one wants children . . . I just thought I'd tell you . . . that, it's hard work, yes, but there are rewards too. I can't imagine life without my children." The woman smiled at her, turned to her locker, picked up her things. "Have a nice day." Elaine Vogt left.

Val stared after her, her hand still protective over her middle. "What will you be, I wonder?" Val asked the growing life inside her. "Are you something now?" She smiled to herself, all at once anxious for Dan to know so that she could tell others.

It was on the walk home that the disquieting thought hit her. She stopped walking for a moment, Henderson pausing at her side. "Is it true that a man's timing in sports can be damaged if he has something on his mind? If he is told something that upsets him?"

Henderson watched her for a moment, then nodded slowly. "It's better to have your mind free to concentrate on the matter at hand. If you're quarterbacking a football team, concentration and timing are integral factors."

Val nodded.

That morning when she went to the station, the celebrity guest was an obnoxious late night comedian who interspersed his responses with salty witticisms that Val found heavy and boring.

It took all her strength of will not to tell the paunchy egotist what she really thought of him. Much of her cool facade was being eroded by pregnancy, and she found it easier and easier to let a simmering temperament erupt.

By the time the show was completed, she was perspiring freely and her clothes stuck to her.

"Val, baby, are you coming down with the flu or something?" Dean glanced at her warily. "If you are, keep your distance. I can't afford to be sick right now."

"Who can?" Val quizzed, more weary than she cared to admit. She went to the ladies' room and took her small vitamin bottle from her purse, taking the vitamin C and multiple vitamin that had been prescribed for her by Dr. Cross.

Later, sitting at her desk and munching an apple, she tried to work on her script for the next day, but she kept seeing Dan's face. When the phone rang, she thought it might be him and she answered it eagerly.

"Well, you sound better than the last time we talked. Is it because the behemoth is in California?" Binkie asked her.

"Binkie, if you were with me," Val ventured sweetly, "I'd grind my spike heel into your instep."

"Val . . . you have become a primitive." Binkie inhaled. "It is most unattractive."

"Stop it. What did you want?" Val snapped.

"John Dewey suggested that the three of us have dinner to decide if it would make a good show to interview the owners of a football team—"

"I did that in New York." Val was abrupt. "It was not that interesting. There is no need of me being there. You can tell John my feelings."

"Val . . . your career is hooked, cheek by jowl, with the well-tailored Mr. Dewey," Binkie pointed out smoothly.

115

"So? If you don't like my answer, confer with Dean. He's the last word on show personalities."

"Valentina, do I detect a burning-thy-bridges tone to your voice?"

"Binkie, I think I once told you that you do not have the credentials to psychoanalyze me. So . . . bug off," Val finished curtly.

"All right, all right, calm down. If you don't want to have dinner, I won't force you . . ."

"You couldn't," Val stated.

"So . . . have drinks with us instead. The Purple Pompom at five?"

"Where is this place?"

"Right around the corner from the Twin Towers. Many of the studio people go there."

"All right. I'll try to get out of here early. If not, start without me."

"Val . . . now . . . listen."

"Good-bye, Binkie." Val replaced the phone on the cradle and tried to get back into her script again. When the phone rang, she was sure it was Dan and answered quickly.

"You do answer your phone fast, I'll say that."

"Binkie! What in—"

"Simmer down. I forgot something." He took a deep breath, further inciting Val's temper. "I talked to Trevor the other day. He was in a tizzy because of what he termed the 'unconscionable seducing of his family away from him by that maternal harridan, Emma Cravick.' It seems Trevor thinks she's engineering a marriage between you and Cravick so that she can get her hands on his money."

"My father is in left field if he thinks that. Emma Cravick could buy and sell him ten times over," Val pronounced, her fingers crossed, since she had no idea of how wealthy the Cravicks were.

"Really? Have you checked this, Val?" Binkie had a wary hope in his voice. "That makes me feel better, since

116

the Cravicks have purchased the LaRue half of the Titans and are now my partners."

"What?" Val jerked upright in her chair.

"Didn't you know? Yes, it seems that they have been pressuring LaRue for some time and finally convinced him. I didn't put up any opposition, but I must say I feel better about having them in my ball park after talking to you. I had visions of going down the tube with my football in my hand," Binkie stated. "Trevor hates 'em, you know."

"Trevor hates anyone who doesn't bleed California blue blood," Val grated. "He is living like an out-of-date Californio . . . and God knows he doesn't have the papers for it."

"Val . . . are you going to marry Cravick?"

"Yes."

"Oh, God, here comes another earthquake. Trevor will blow this town apart when he hears."

"Are you going to tell him, chum?" Val asked.

"Not me! I never willingly endanger my existence." Binkie paused. "What made you change your mind, Val? I didn't think you would ever change your mind."

"Circumstances." Val hung up the phone.

117

## CHAPTER SEVEN

The scrimmage game with the San Francisco Forty-Niners occurred on a very warm, sunshiny day in Candlestick Park, the usual windstorm blowing there.

Val was surprised by the crowds, not expecting such a group at a mere scrimmage game before the real season had begun. When she mentioned this to Binkie, he shrugged.

"That's San Francisco, the city of enthusiasm." Binkie grinned at her as he gestured to Carol and Les to take the row behind him, Val, and the Cravicks and next to Trevor, Michael, and Ruth. Trevor was still stiff-lipped about coming. "Stay out here and live permanently, and you'll see how warm-blooded Californians are about anything and everything."

"I was born out here, Binkie. Remember?" Val said dryly. She looked around her. "I must say I can't fault the seating arrangements. I have never been so close to the field."

"You were when you saw Dan play in Pasadena," Binkie pointed out, his tone matching hers.

Val nodded. "I guess you're right." She glanced quickly back at her father meaning to say something to him but intimidated by his granite expression.

"He saw that rock on your finger," Binkie hissed.

"So?" Val's voice held bravado; her insides were jelly. She dreaded the scene that she would have to face with her father.

Michael leaned down to her. "Les and I have told Trevor that we approve of Dan as a brother-in-law."

Val sighed and turned to smile at her brother. "Thanks."

Michael leaned even closer, so that his mouth was close to her ear. "Ruth and Carol think you should tell Dan your news." He watched her blandly when she gaped at him. "Have you told him?"

Val looked from him to her smiling sister and sister-in-law, then shook her head, earning three frowns from her relatives. "No."

"Tell him, Val," Michael urged, sitting back and answering a terse remark of his father's.

The roar of the stadium announced the entrance of the San Francisco team and a few boos and loud applause from Binkie's box heralded the New York Titans.

"Throw that bum Cravick out. He's no quarterback," a loud voice from above them shouted.

Val surged to her feet, turning round to face the enemy, aware of her father's horrified look and the bemused looks of the Cravicks and the others. "You shut your mouth or I'll sock you right in the nose," said Miss Rogers of the Villeneuve Finishing School for Ladies of Breeding.

A mocking answer was cut off when a group of men looked down and saw the delicately boned, high-fashioned blonde glaring up at them.

"Hey . . . quiet, Joe. That's Cravick's old lady." A booming whisper floated down to them in the sudden quiet before the national anthem.

"Valentina . . ." Her father's tone was brimstone.

"Valentina is right." Yanos bellowed, his stance warlike as he looked around him.

"Isn't she sweet?" Emma turned around and cooed to Trevor, making Carol and Ruth bury their faces in their hands, shoulders shaking.

"Have some champagne, sir?" Binkie rallied, handing

119

Trevor a tulip glass of bubbly, glaring at Val at the same time.

Les and Michael gladly helped Binkie open the wine.

After the kickoff, Val didn't notice much around her. She groaned, flinched, winced, at each offensive play of the Titans, and craned her neck to watch Dan when he was on the bench. He never looked up to the box, his concentration on the play total and all-encompassing.

The teams were well matched, and they surged up and down the field, trying not to give an inch. By the end of the first quarter the teams were still 0 to 0. In the second quarter the classy quarterback on the Forty-Niners threw a bullet pass into the end zone, and the kicker converted the point, making the score Forty-Niners 7, Titans 0 to the ecstatic roars of the heavily San Francisco crowd.

When Dan faded back to throw a screen pass, it seemed to Val that all the Forty-Niners sacked him, not just two defensemen from San Francisco.

"No . . ." Val jumped to her feet, thumping Binkie on the shoulder with her fist. "Stop that. You'll hurt him." She turned around to glare at Les when she heard him laughing.

"Sorry, Val . . . but he is all right." Les spread his hands, rubbing his arm when his wife punched him.

Second down and fifteen, Dan faded back to pass, saw an opening and started running up the field. . . . The crowd was on its feet, screaming, moaning, cheering, as Dan pummeled down the field, raging behemoths at his heels.

"No . . . no . . . don't catch him . . . don't catch him . . ." Val was screaming, tearing at the cloth of Binkie's jacket.

"Val, for God's sake . . . oh Lord, look at him go. . . . I think . . . I think . . ." Binkie was stuttering, craning his neck, yelling louder than Val, "Touchdown . . . touchdown . . . he did it . . . he did it . . ."

Pandemonium reigned as even Trevor was on his feet

ringing Yanos's hand as the two men grinned from ear to ear.

"What a run . . . what a run . . ." Petros kept repeating, shaking his head, patting his sister-in-law on the shoulder as she dabbed at her eyes with her hankie.

Val stared down the field as Dan walked off surrounded by teammates pounding his shoulders, jumping up and down. She felt frozen to the spot when he suddenly looked up, searched the crowd, found her, and grinned. Dan, Dan, Dan, Dan . . . the name echoed in her mind as she watched the Titans' kicker, a former soccer player, send the ball between the uprights to score the conversion. The score was now 7 to 7 at the end of the first half.

Val didn't even watch the half-time show that had the rest of them cheering and sighing.

"My goodness, Val, if Dan watches those gorgeous cheerleaders all the time, he must be goggle-eyed." Carol chuckled when Val turned to glare at her. "What bodies they have! Lester, close your eyes."

Ruth leaned down to pat Val on the shoulder. "Pay no attention to Michael and Les. You know how men have to drool over such stuff."

Val smiled weakly, stared at the Titanettes in their minuscule costumes, pressed her tummy, and groaned. Why couldn't the cheerleaders be ugly, have cross-eyes, and thick ankles, flat chests and no derrieres?

Val looked around and saw that her father had taken Binkie's place when the other man had gone to talk to Petros and Emma Cravick. "Hello, father." Val's nervousness disappeared as she stared at her father. If he said one word against Dan, she would . . . she would . . . She could feel her hands close into fists.

"Val . . . I see you are determined to marry this Cravick."

"I am."

"Then I must ask you to learn a little restraint. It is most unseemly for a Rogers or a Gilmartin to threaten to

121

hit someone at a football game." Trevor fixed her with a gimlet eye.

Val's mouth opened and closed. She had not expected him to say that. "Ah . . . well . . . I don't intend to do it . . . you see . . ."

"Restraint, Val, that's the secret. Try to remember that."

"Yes, Father," Val mumbled.

The kickoff at the start of the second half was a long spiraling ball deep into Titan territory. The running back who brought the ball down the field was a stranger to Val, but she was on her feet cheering.

The two teams fought back and forth through the third and fourth quarters, the score staying at 7 to 7.

When Dan had the ball in the final minutes of the game and threw to a receiver who missed it, Binkie's entire box groaned. There was a penalty on the play, and so it was third down and seventeen for a first down. The linebackers charged across the middle seeking to sack the quarterback again. Still running, Dan looked and fired the ball like a missile downfield. The man receiving was the bull-like Bear Dulane, who Dan had described to Val as being a good man to plunge through the middle for the short gain.

Screaming at the top of her lungs, Ruth and Carol jumped up and down on their seats, their husbands roaring approval. Even Trevor was on his feet.

Val could hear Emma Cravick calling to Bear to hurry as the burly man, showing surprising knee-up running speed, plowed down the sidelines to the end zone to score and trigger the wildly screaming gathering for the Titans.

Val never took her eyes off the pile of men who had bulled down the quarterback. One by one they peeled away until she saw Dan crouched on the ground.

He didn't get up at once.

Val moaned to herself. He's hurt, he's hurt!

Dan got up and started running toward Bear, who had

122

just thrown the ball to the ground in the end zone and was immediately surrounded by his own teammates.

A shaken Val joined in the cheering as the point was converted and time ran out, Titans winning 14 to 7.

Dan ran off the field toward their seats, waving to them, his face grinning and sweat-streaked hair plastered to his forehead, looking right at Val. In seconds there were people around him, including two young, well-developed women who tried to reach up and kiss him.

"Hussies," Ruth muttered behind Val.

"Football players have their groupies too," Val said in a very normal tone, her fingers itching to get at those women.

"I thought we'd wait for Dan at my apartment, if you like, Val . . ."

"No . . . ah . . . why not go to the house on Lombard Street. Henderson has prepared something . . . and I know Dan will be tired. I'll wait for him . . . you go ahead."

"I don't think she should wait here by herself . . ." Trevor began.

"Don't be silly, Father. I'll be fine."

She waited in Binkie's box, watching in desultory fashion as the grounds keepers for Candlestick Park moved right into action to remedy whatever damage had been done there that day.

"Hi."

Startled, Val looked around to see Bear Dulane waiting there, his hair still wet from his shower. "Hi, yourself." Val smiled at the giant of a man. "Congratulations on that touchdown. It was great." Val had not been watching Bear at all, but she wanted to congratulate him.

"Thanks, Val. Dan had his interview after me, so he said to tell you he'll be right along. Are you coming to the party, Val?" Bear grinned at her, the flush of victory still on his face.

"Ah . . . I'm not sure. We were supposed to meet our folks back at the house. . . ." Val fumbled.

"Ah, come Val. You'll be the prettiest one at the party. Just for a little while. Hey . . . Dan. I was trying to talk Val into coming to the party . . . for just a little while."

Val looked around at her conquering hero, seeing the stance of the winner in the set of his shoulders, the sapphire sheen to his eyes as he looked at her. "Hello, darling." He bent to kiss her, not a peck, but a deep searching caress that made Bear laugh and whistle. "Would you mind if we went for just a minute, then went to Binkie's?"

"Everyone is at the house . . . won't Binkie want to be at this party?"

Dan shrugged. "I don't know. It's just the guys getting together to tip a few."

Val nodded. "All right, but we should call." She could tell that Dan was still keyed to playing pitch and probably needed to wind down with his teammates. She couldn't understand the prickling uneasiness that ran over her skin.

Dan called the house and told them that he and Val would be a little late in arriving.

The party was in a private home near the outskirts of the city. The hostess was a cousin of one of the players and seemed to be on the wealthy side.

Val hung back, the brash noisy gathering of players and people stifling her in the confines of the house. She felt a queasiness in the heat and smoke that made her slightly light-headed.

The woman, Diana Walker, came and took hold of Dan. "You don't mind if I borrow him for a moment, do you?"

"I'll be right back, honey." Dan was excited by the win. As Val watched him work his way across the room, talking to his friends and acquaintances, she could see how happy he was with his friends; her heart lurched as she felt more and more out of place. She spoke to several persons, then Bear Dulane was at her side again.

"Bear, do you think you might mention to Dan that I think I'll meet him back at the house. . . ." Val thanked

Bear when he accompanied her to the phone and waited while she called a cab. Then he walked her out the front door and down the steps to the waiting taxi.

She stared unseeing out the glass windows at the houses passing by, feeling only relief when the car pulled up in front of the house on Lombard Street.

She was about to turn away after paying the cab when Dan screeched up to the curb, cramped his wheels, got out, and stared at her tight-lipped. "Why didn't you tell me that you wanted to leave? Why did Bear have to tell me that you didn't feel good? Why didn't you tell me yourself?"

"Where were you?" Val snapped back, her temper fraying. "If you had been around, I would have told you."

"Val . . . listen . . ."

"No, you listen . . ." She tugged and panted trying to pull the ring from her finger.

"Stop it." Dan closed his big hand around hers, stopping her movements. "That ring stays on there. I'm sorry. I shouldn't have left you alone. I don't know why . . ."

"You did it because you wanted to be with your friends, the ones who were with you when you won the game. You needed that." Val swallowed. "I don't belong in that life, Dan. We can't kid ourselves about that."

"You belong anywhere that I am." He pulled her close to him, his arm staying at her waist as they climbed the steps to the front door.

Henderson opened it, and Perro was there to welcome them. "Your father is annoyed that you have an animal, Miss Val. He says they are dirty and that he wouldn't allow them in his home." He winked one of his satchel eyes at her.

"Lord, I suppose he has been giving you a hard time." Val smiled at her friend, turning to look at Dan and freezing where she stood.

His face was twisted with anger, and his hands hung at his sides, opening and closing.

"What is it? What's wrong?" Val whispered, looking over her shoulder to see if anyone in the lounge had noticed that she and Dan were in the foyer.

Henderson looked from one to the other, took the dog by the collar, and went to the kitchen.

Val looked up at Dan. "What is it?"

"You are always full of smiles with any man but me . . . even with the Bear . . . always smiling, always charming . . ." Dan ground out the words.

Val stamped her foot on the parquet floor. "Don't be an ass. I—"

"Ah, there you are, Danilo. Fine job today." Yanos Cravick came out to the foyer and took hold of his nephew in a bear hug that would have broken the bones of most men. "We are waiting for you . . . to celebrate with the champagne. . . ." Yanos screwed up his face. "It is not as good as the ouzo I make . . . but it pleases your mother."

"Ouzo would put me away." Dan patted his uncle on the back, then stood back, gesturing for Val to precede him into the lounge.

Greetings and congratulations kept Dan busy as Val's brother and brother-in-law seemed to go over every play that Dan had made.

"When I saw you fade back and then that huge lineman came at you . . . what's his name . . ." Michael waxed enthusiastic.

"DeCarolis, Clem DeCarolis . . ." Dan tipped some of the champagne into his mouth, smiling. "He's big . . . and fast . . ."

Val made a move away from Dan and felt one of his strong arms go around her waist. "Ah . . . I thought I would get something to drink." She was still angry at what Dan had said to her, but a part of her agreed with him. It was easier for her to talk to any other man. With Dan she always felt as though she must hide some of herself,

126

put up a fence to protect herself from the hurt she knew that Dan could give her.

"Here . . . drink from my glass . . ." Dan curled her closer to her, putting his glass to her lips.

"She shouldn't drink so much," Yanos bellowed.

"You were the one giving her drinks the other evening," Dan shot back, his hand tightening on Val's shoulder.

"I did not know then that Valentina is to have a baby." He glared from Petros to Emma. "And if I did not hear your mama whispering to my brother, I would not know it yet," Yanos finished, not seeming to notice the dead silence that followed his words.

Val felt sick. She couldn't look at Dan, whose arm had dropped from her shoulder. She felt an hysterical laugh bubble up in her at Binkie's mouth opening and closing like a gaffed fish. He poured himself a full glass of wine and gulped the whole thing.

"Valentina. It isn't true, is it?" Her father rasped.

"Leave Val alone," Carol said as she and Ruth moved toward her, Emma in their wake.

"Yanos, Yanos, why did you have to say something?" Emma snapped, wringing her hands as she stood in front of Val. "It's my fault, dear. I shouldn't have said anything to Petros. No one else knew . . ."

"We knew." Ruth put her arm around Val. "Carol and I and Les and Michael. . . ."

"Is it true?" Dan whirled on Val, his roar blowing out the windows for miles around, Val was sure.

The silence stretched until Valentina thought she might scream, Dan's tension effectively gagging other comment.

"It's true." Val cleared her throat, looking up at him, thinking how large he was, bone and muscle straining against the light denim suit he was wearing.

"When the hell were you going to tell me?" The words hissed like live steam from his mouth.

"When we had time . . . to talk . . ." Val tried to explain, but no words came.

127

"I'm listening." Dan thrust his face forward, making Trevor Rogers take one step back and Binkie gulp more wine.

It occurred to Val that Binkie liked wine just a little less than beer, and she turned to him. "Shall I get Henderson to get you some Irish whiskey?" Her mind seemed to have lost its ability to retain. It was blank.

"For me?" Binkie stared from her to Dan goggle-eyed. "No. Just fine. Love champagne."

"You hate champagne," Val reminded him.

"Stop that," Dan bellowed

All at once everyone sat down, leaving only Dan and Val standing.

Val glared at him. "Stop shouting. You made Binkie spill his wine."

"Too damn bad," Dan said, one decibel lower.

"Couldn't agree more," Binkie said, gulping more wine.

"We're getting married tonight." Dan's head swung around the room like a smashing ball on a derrick.

Every head in the room but Val's and her father's was nodding.

When Dan inhaled and stared at Trevor Rogers, he nodded once too.

"Oh dear, I do hate it when Dan gets this way," Emma explained to a fascinated Ruth. "He can be a tad unruly, can't he, Petros?"

"Yes." Dan's uncle relaxed in his chair, his eyes clinically observing his most irate nephew.

"You should have been married to her a long time ago," Yanos barked. "Why did you tell me he was married to this woman, Emma?"

"Because it was easier than listening to you bawl like the Bulls of Bashan because you didn't approve of Dan's life-style." Emma pursed her lips at her brother-in-law.

"I do not approve of him living with this Valentina. She carrying his child, no less. He must marry her," Yanos stated, making the drapes sway at the window.

"We're flying to Las Vegas tonight and getting married . . . so you can forget the lecture, Uncle Yanos." Dan spat the words.

His uncle stared at him. "You are much angry, Danilo."

"Much."

Val opened her mouth to say something, and Dan rounded on her, his arm outstretched.

"Not a *single* word, Val, unless you want me to take this town apart brick by damn brick. I mean it. We're flying to Nevada and getting married . . . as soon as I can charter a plane."

"Perhaps we could all go . . ." Emma began only to be shushed by Petros and the thunderous look of her son. "Well, I only thought . . ."

"If you knew about this, why didn't you tell me?" Dan's voice still penetrated like a drill through concrete.

His mother sat straighter. "What did you think was making Val's tummy so round? Melon seeds?"

Dan threw a look at Val's middle, somewhat camouflaged by her jacket, a dark red filling his neck and face. "Damn it, I thought . . . never mind what I thought . . ."

"Well, Danilo, you should take better care of your own. That's all I have to say. Your father would never have let me . . ." Emma stated, making Dan gnash his teeth.

"Valentina should have told him." Trevor stepped into the breech, glowering at his daughter. "Now I suppose they will have to marry . . . for the time being . . ."

"Marriage is for always," Yanos bellowed.

When it looked like the two families would erupt into a full-scale shouting match, Val stepped forward. "I don't want to hear anymore. Dan and I will marry . . . whether the marriage works will be our business . . . no one else's."

Henderson brought food, and though the others ate, Val's stomach could tolerate nothing but the herbal tea that was made especially for her.

Dan escaped to the study, mumbling something about planes and booking a chapel.

Carol and Ruth cried a little when she and Dan left to take a taxi to the airfield where a Cessna was waiting to fly them to Las Vegas.

Val wanted to talk to Dan, but she didn't know where to begin. There was so much misunderstanding between them, and though she knew she should have told him about the baby, she was too proud to say she was sorry, too proud to tell him that she loved him, that she was happy about their baby and wanted to stay with him. That she wanted their marriage to work.

It was evening when they reached the gambling kingdom, and the city dazzled them with her full array of flashing lights.

Dan surprised her by taking her to the chapel first.

"So this is why you wanted me to wear my suit on the plane." Val spoke her first words, tugging at the tight skirt of her apricot satin ensemble that both Carol and Ruth thought perfect for a wedding.

"Yes." Dan handed her up the steps. A liveried messenger came forward with a florist box.

"Mr. Cravick? These are the flowers you ordered. Hey . . . thank you very much." The young man fingered the ten-dollar bill Dan had given him, then watched Dan take the peachy-cream orchid from the box and hand it to Val.

Val held the tussie-mussie containing the orchid in front of her as she and Dan entered the chapel and were introduced to the cleric and the witnesses.

It took mere minutes to make Valentina Rogers Gilmartin Valentina Rogers Gilmartin Cravick. She shook hands with everyone, her plastic smile staying in place even after her husband's peck on the cheek.

When she and Dan went outside as husband and wife, a man was there leaning against a Corvette. He straightened and smiled at Dan. "I didn't believe it when my boss said that Dan Cravick was renting one of our cars. Could

I have your autograph? Gee, Devil Dan Cravick right in front of me. I saw that game last year in the Super Bowl. Great. Are you going to be in the Super Bowl this year?"

"I'm going to try," Dan said mildly, signing his autograph and the car rental agreement, then taking Val's arm and leading her to the Corvette.

"We're staying at Caesar's for the night. Then we'll fly back to San Francisco the next night."

Val held back a sigh, hearing the remoteness in his voice. Dan hadn't forgiven her. "Sounds good."

"I suppose you'll still use the name Gilmartin as your professional name?"

"Ah . . . I suppose." Val clenched her jaw. If he wanted to be noncommunicative, she could be too.

The suite at Caesar's was elegant, perhaps a little too opulent for Val's taste, but still, a kernel of excitement was building in her. She hadn't been to Las Vegas in years. She couldn't remember the last time she'd gambled, considering the pastime boring, but now she wanted to do anything that might distract Dan.

She laughed out loud when she saw the round tub recessed in the middle of the floor.

Dan walked into the bathroom, pulling the tie from around his neck. "What's so funny?"

Val pointed. "The Roman tub. We could have a party in there."

"Why don't we, Mrs Cravick?" Dan saw her move back a step, his black brows bridging over his nose in a frown. "We're married."

"Yes." Val felt the familiar aching warmth build as Dan pulled her into his arms.

"Can I make love to you, Val?" He mumbled into her hair. "I mean . . . I don't want to hurt you."

"Don't be silly, you can make love to me . . . but shouldn't we put our clothes out in the other room." She leaned back to look up into his face, her heart missing a full beat at the heat in those sapphire eyes.

131

"Here's fine." Dan reached over to the wall and turned the faucets to let the flow of water into the tub, then he activated the Jacuzzi switch as well.

He peeled the jacket and blouse from her body, staring down at her full breasts, barely covered by the lacy peach-colored bra. "I knew they were fuller . . . so nice." He bent his head, nuzzled aside the lace, and took one nipple into his mouth.

# CHAPTER EIGHT

That evening when she and Dan dressed to eat and gamble, she felt different toward Dan . . . a shyness, a reserve. It was as though their lovemaking had been new, as though he had never held her body in his arms and loved every inch of her.

Her body had reacted to him in the same automatic way, but there had been a shading to it, a nuance that puzzled Val. She shook her head to clear it of such silly thoughts and tried to concentrate on her mirror image. She frowned at her round tummy.

"Don't pat your abdomen and frown at it." Dan came up behind her, his arms going around her to cover hers, his eyes burning over her partially nude form. "You're lovely, Val. Your platinum hair and golden eyes are so perfect." He muttered the words. "How do you think this looks against that white skin?" Dan reached back into his pocket and took out a strand of pearls. He smiled at her, then lifted her hair and fixed the string of gems to her throat. "Earrings too. See?" He held the dangling pearls, held by a short rope of gold in front of her. "Happy wedding day, Mrs. Cravick."

"Dan, they're beautiful." She grinned at herself after she affixed the earrings. Now she stood in bikini panties and pearls. "I look like a slave on the market."

"I'd buy you any day." Dan kissed her neck, then noticed the goose bumps on her skin. "You're cold. Here, let

133

me help you with your dress." He didn't see Val bite her lip.

How could she tell Dan that what made her skin cold was the thought that someday he might leave her, and though it would be some consolation to have his child, her life would still be empty without him in it. There would still be a void. Dan had filled her . . . had made her complete . . . had allowed her to be a woman of courage because his love allowed her to dare all things. She would tell him none of this; she would not try to hold him because of her deep emotional commitment to him. Pride wouldn't let her do that.

Memory shook her as she recalled what Dan's uncle had said about pride.

"Pride squeezes love, flaws it, cuts it, and leaves it to die."

"Val? Val, pay attention. Is this the way this dress goes?"

"Huh? Oh . . . yes . . . that's the front . . ." Val lifted her arms to help Dan ease the dress down the front of her. It was one of the few evening dresses that she owned that could mask her pregnant figure. It was strapless, all the fullness gathered under the bust, to fall in layers to her calf in front and down to floor level in the tapered back. The tissue silk in antique gold color floated around her body, the pearls iridescent against her white skin. "Does the dress camouflage my curves?"

"I notice it, but I don't think anyone else will be looking. I just thought you had gained a few pounds . . ." Dan shook his head. "Since you were on your pills, I never thought you might be pregnant."

"I stopped using them . . . but if the doctor is correct, I became pregnant while I thought I was still using them." Val shrugged.

"When is our baby due?" Dan took hold of her upper arms, caressing the bare skin with his fingertips.

134

Val felt her mouth drop open. "That's right. You don't know, do you?"

"I don't know anything," Dan said gruffly. "That's why I'm asking."

Val bit her lip, a wriggle of guilt deep inside her. She hadn't really discussed the baby with anyone save the doctor, but Dan should have known. "Dr. Cross says the baby is due in January."

"January?" Dan's computation was done in seconds. "You were on the pill when you conceived, then." He frowned for a minute, then smiled. "It seems you're a very fertile lady."

"It would seem you're a very virile man," she shot back.

He laughed and picked her up in his arms so that they were eye to eye. "And are you well? Does the doctor say that you can carry this baby without problem?"

"Everything looks good, she said. Of course, there is always the chance of something unexpected, but I'm so healthy that I'm not worried and neither is the doctor."

"She? You have a woman doctor out here too?"

"Yes. Don't you approve?"

"Of course I approve. I want you to be comfortable with the physician attending you." Dan kissed her cheek.

Val thought she heard him say her name, but when he leaned back and smiled at her, she thought she must be mistaken.

Dan lowered her to the floor. "You must be hungry. I made reservations for dinner in the hotel dining room . . . then if you like, we'll gamble."

"You know I don't know anything about gambling." Val felt her heart flip over when he bent and kissed her cheek after locking their suite door.

"If you don't like it, we won't do it."

"You could teach me," Val said hurriedly, feeling that gambling would be safer than the many questions that Dan could ask her.

They weren't in the dining room five minutes when Val

135

noticed the murmurs going round the room. Dan had been recognized! It had happened to them too many times for Val not to be cognizant of it. Dan kept on eating the shrimp cocktail he had ordered as an appetizer.

Val took a few spoonfuls of her vegetable soup and pushed it to one side.

"Honey? Eat your soup. It's good for you."

"It makes me feel uneasy . . . the staring. . . ." she finished as he looked at her, one eyebrow raised.

He glanced once around the room then back at Val. "Ignore it. I do."

"I know."

He hitched his chair around closer to her, his big body acting as a screen for Val from the rest of the room. "Better?"

"Yes." Val picked up her spoon, then set it down again.

It surprised her when Dan picked up her spoon, lifting it toward her. "Open."

Too shocked to protest, Val opened her mouth and took the soup from the spoon. She took three more, then put her hand on his. "This is silly." She felt more carefree than she had felt for so long . . . since she had come out to California.

"You finished most of it." Dan smiled at her, then spooned the rest of the soup into his own mouth. "My mother taught me not to leave food."

'I'll bet you ate her out of house and home, as the saying goes." Val relaxed in her chair. The soup had warmed her and though the temperature outside was on the hot side, she had been unable to shake off a chill feeling since their marriage.

"I was always hungry." Dan leaned over and lifted her left hand, kissing the ring finger, then biting on her fingers. "But this is my favorite food."

"Me?" Val laughed, feeling like a girl.

'You. I could eat you up. You know that."

136

Val felt as though she had disappeared into Dan's eyes, that she was sliding down into his being.

When the waiter placed the chicken roulade in front of her, she jumped. The spell was broken.

They took a long time over their meal. Val's appetite was better than it had been in a long time. The rolled chicken breast stuffed with carrot and green pepper was fork-tender and aromatic.

Dan finished her saffron rice and all of the bread. He ordered cheese and fruit for dessert; Val ordered herbal tea. "Do you really like that?"

"Henderson started me on it. Coffee and regular tea made me queasy . . ." Val's voice trailed off when she saw Dan's eyebrows snap together. She coughed. "Henderson has been a friend to me since I was a young girl. I was always a hell-raiser, as Michael will be glad to tell you. Once I coerced my brother and Binkie to take me to one of those illegal boxing matches they used to hold at those private clubs . . ."

Dan shook his head. "Never went to one."

"They used to have them here . . . well, I mean in California. I watched the fight and was almost sick. The man they put in the ring opposite the 'champion' was obviously too old, and over the hill for boxing. He was smashed." Val choked, bit her lip. "I had won a bet with Binkie that I would be able to get Michael to take me to anything I chose. Binkie let me pick the prize. We took Henderson, who was the beaten fighter, to the doctor, then we took him to Binkie's house on Lombard Street and told him it was his job to take care of the house. . . ."

"You might say that you bought him with the house. Is that it?" Dan said softly.

"You could say that . . . except that Henderson couldn't be owned by anyone. He's a good and honest man. I saw that when he was being pummeled against the ropes in the ring. . . ."

137

"So that's why he looks at you in that fierce way he has."

"Does he?" Val was startled. "I never noticed. He's just a good friend. I was never able to talk to my own father. Henderson always listened."

Dan nodded, then stood and pulled back her chair. "How would you like to see the cabaret and dance a little before gambling?"

"Fine."

Val braced herself before walking into the nightclub, and of course Dan was recognized, but since his arm was around her, his body protective, she felt strong.

The show was bawdy all the way through, amusing in bits and pieces.

Val was relieved when the show ended, but then a chorus line of scantily clad beauties danced out under a hot pink light, their long legs and curvaceous bodies flashing sensually in front of the customers.

When the girl who seemed to be the lead dancer came over to Dan and put a scarf around his neck and tugged, he just smiled and shook his head.

Rage shook Val from ankle to ear. Her hand clenched around the seltzer and lime in a glass in front of her. She would pour it down the hussy's cleavage.

"You don't mind if we take your famous boyfriend for a moment, do you, sweetie?" the busty brunette simpered at Val, still tugging at Dan.

"If you mean my husband, that's up to him." Val could feel her smile slipping.

Dan laughed. "I don't think I want to go up on stage." He smiled at the brunette, who was almost lying across him now.

"Well, would you just stand up?" She looked up at the audience from her vantage point on Dan's chest. "Folks, this is Dan Cravick. Wouldn't you like him to take a bow on stage?"

There was applause and cheering as Dan lifted the brunette from his lap and stood, waving to the audience. He made no move to go up on the stage.

When the girl saw that she wasn't going to move Dan, she reached up with both hands and caught his face, pulling it down so that she kissed him right on the mouth . . . not a short kiss either, but a prolonged smack.

Val felt as though all her teeth had welded together in her mouth, blood pumping through her, as she decided at that very moment that she was going to back a car over the brunette *and* Dan.

To hoots and catcalls the kiss was broken, and the girl joined her dancing teammates. Dan laughed and sat down, taking a hankie from his pocket and wiping his mouth before glancing at Val. He watched her warily. "It isn't like that all the time."

"I should hope not." Val kept smiling, though her face hurt.

"I didn't expect that, Valentina. You must know that I didn't like it anymore than you did, but I didn't want to make a scene."

"Oh, I think you enjoyed it a bit more than I did, Danilo," Val offered.

The show ended and the dancing began. When Dan gestured to her, she rose and preceded him out to the floor.

His body screened her from the room. "Don't be angry, Val."

"I'm not angry . . . just . . . just disgusted." Val tried to get the squeak out of her voice.

Dan enfolded her close to him, his large frame moving in easy rhythm to the music. It never ceased to amaze Val that he could be so light on his feet on a dance floor and be such a bull on the football field.

"It's been a long time since we danced." Dan's voice was a husky whisper into her hair.

"It's been a long time since we did anything together," Val said on a shaky sigh.

His arms tightened on her. "I hate us to be apart, Val.

139

Are you going to stay in San Francisco when I go back to New York?"

Val stiffened in his arms, her thoughts going round and round. She had no ready answer. "No." The word was out before she had conjured the thought. "No . . . I don't think the station will want me when I begin to fill out." Val gave a half laugh.

Dan's hands clenched on her body. "So, for whatever reason . . . you'll be coming back to New York?"

"Yes." Val felt his chest expand under her cheek.

"Good."

The music changed to a sweet rock and roll sound, the faster rhythm appealing to Val all at once.

When Dan tried to lead her from the floor, she balked, freed herself from him and began the body gyration that matched the music.

"Val! Is it all right?" Dan hissed at her.

"Of course." She didn't pause, the motion carrying her around Dan's body.

He watched her warily for a few seconds.

"Hey, Devil Dan. If you don't want to dance with her, I will."

Dan reached out a hand to scoop Val closer to his body, his angry growl penetrating the sounds of the music as he searched the crowd for the man who had called out to him.

No one came forward.

"Dan . . . free me a little. We don't dance this close to this type of music." Val couldn't help laughing at the bulldog look on his face. How strange it was! She never feared Dan in the least, never felt the smallest physical or mental intimidation even when he was in a fury. He wasn't in a rage at the moment, but he was irritated by what the man had said to him. Val looked around her too, wondering who had said it.

"Why don't we gamble for a while?" Val suggested.

"Did the dancing tire you?" Dan searched her face.

"No . . . I just thought it might be fun . . ." She paused, grinning at him. "I just thought it might be safer than starting a fight in the nightclub."

Dan's slow grin pulled Val to pieces. "Right. The bastard. I felt like shaking him . . . wherever the hell he is . . ." Dan's head swiveled round the dance floor.

"Never mind him." Val tugged at his hand. It closed around hers at once.

Dan settled the bill, then curved his arm around Val, leading her from the room, not seeming to notice the eyes that followed him.

Val saw them. It was always like this, she recalled, from the moment they met. Someone was bound to recognize Dan. She looked up at him and caught him looking down at her. She smiled, feeling a strange peace, a comfort.

Dan played baccarat. He tried to explain it to Val, but she just didn't understand it.

She wandered away when she noticed that he was engrossed, thinking that a show on gambling, how gamblers feel, the compulsive gambler, might make a very interesting episode on the talk show.

She watched the dice throwers for a short time. When a man said "Your dice, lady," and handed them to her, she threw them inside the long coffinlike box.

"The lady's point is four." A man in a black suit with a croupier's stick in his hand pulled the dice back toward her again. She threw again and won. She knew it because the man told her so. She put down some chips, her Scottish blood rebelling at wasting money on the roll of the dice. It was exhilarating to win, but she refused to place any more than one chip on a roll. Not so the people around her. As she continued to win, the crowd grew around her and more money was thrown on the table.

She waited a moment, not all the urgings of the persons hanging over the table making her throw. "Do all these people lose if I do?" she whispered out the side of her mouth to the attendant standing there.

"Yes, ma'am. Your dice."

"Good Lord." Val threw a seven and lost, her hands perspiring, not looking up as she surrendered the ivories to the next roller. She swung around right into Dan's chest. "That was awful," she muttered into his shirt.

"Why?" His chest heaved with laughter. "You were winning for a while."

Val lifted her head, smiling at him. "Oh, did you see it?"

"Yes. As soon as I realized that you weren't standing behind me, I came looking for you."

"Oh, Dan, you shouldn't have. I didn't understand what you were doing, so I thought I'd look around. Gambling might be a good idea for a show. What do you think?"

"I thought you said that the network wouldn't let you stay when you began to show." There was a tension to the strong arms that held her.

"Well . . . not that, really. I suppose they would keep me, even though I haven't signed a long-term contract . . . but I think they would be more comfortable with someone not pregnant . . . and I would be more comfortable working behind the cameras. New York said that they might let me direct a few shows. . . ." She shrugged.

"Would you like that?" Dan stopped when she did so that she could watch the blackjack game.

"I don't know. I'll see how I feel."

Dan nodded, his eyes having a hooded look to them. "Would you like to play blackjack?"

"I hate losing," Val whispered, watching the quick deal of cards. "It was awful back there when the man told me that when I lost all the people lost too."

Dan shrugged. "They know it when they put their money down."

Val studied him while he looked round the room, his tall, strong body standing out among the throngs of people. His craggy good looks unmarred by his long career in one of the toughest of the contact sports, he had a sensual

142

look to him that nothing could disguise. Just looking at him made Val's knees weak. "Dan?"

He looked down at her in inquiry, the lazy heat in his eyes assessing her. "What?"

"Would you like to play blackjack?"

"No."

"What then?"

Dan looked at her, inhaling a deep breath. "I'd like to take my wife back to our suite and make love to her." His voice was casual.

"Really?" Val squeaked, not able to master the aplomb that was second nature to Dan.

"Really."

"Well . . ." Val looked around her at the feverish activity of the gamblers, feeling a shyness with Dan that she had noticed before when they were in their rooms. She had never even felt the slightest reserve with him from the moment of their first meeting. Why would this silliness afflict her now when she was married to the man? ". . . ah . . . don't let me stop you."

Dan slipped his arm round her, folding her close to his body, turning her toward the door.

Val looked up at him, but there was nothing to see on that enigmatic face. Years of masking his emotions while a ton-weight of men charged at him stood him in good stead now as he strode through the gambling room to the foyer, nodding to those who called out to him, but never slackening his speed.

"Dan . . . I feel like I'm flying. . . ." Val gasped.

"It's all right, darling, I won't let you fall." He looked down at her, narrow-eyed. "Shall I carry you now?"

Val gazed wildly at the crowds of people milling about and shook her head. "Never. Just slow down a bit."

Dan's speed slackened at once. "Sorry, love. I guess I'm too anxious."

"I'm anxious myself," Val answered.

Dan's body jerked and he stopped dead. When Val

143

looked up at him, she saw streaks of red run up his cheeks. It delighted her to throw him off stride because it was a rare occurrence.

"Val . . . you won't be sleeping tonight," Dan muttered, then started down the corridor to their suite of rooms.

"Bragger." She giggled as he pushed open the door and urged her inside.

"Bragger, am I?" Dan stood, legs apart, his hands hanging loosely, a reckless grin on his face. "Challenging me, wife?"

"Yep." Val thumped him on the chest with her fist.

"Little devil." He swept her up in his strong arms, striding toward the bedroom. "We're going to have our Jacuzzi first, then . . ."

"I thought we did that," she murmured into his neck.

"We didn't, but now we will. God, you excite me."

Val lifted her head from his shoulder just before he let her stand. "Did I tell you that pregnant women are very sexy?"

"No, I don't think you told me that, but I must say I'm grateful to you for telling me. I'll make sure that I take more naps from now until January."

"And what does that mean?" Val watched him suspiciously as he unhooked her stockings and rolled them down her leg.

Dan looked up at her and chuckled. "It means that you were always a sensualist, lady mine. You always met me more than halfway in our love play and that now you'll probably have me in a hospital in January right along with you. . . . Ouch, stop pulling my hair." Dan laughed from his kneeling position in front of her, leaning forward to kiss her instep as he edged the sheer nylon from it. "You have the greatest legs, and I do love them." He looked up at her, his soft blue eyes hot and probing. "But when did you start wearing a garter belt and stockings instead of panty hose?"

"Panty hose were beginning to itch my skin. See"—Val

144

pointed to her bare middle—"I'm starting to get stretch marks. Dr. Cross told me it's because my hips are small . . . so I'm stretching out instead of wide."

Dan was still. "Is that bad?"

"No, silly, not all women are built the same."

"You can say that again." Dan kissed her abdomen. "No one is built like you, angel. That's the first thing I noticed about you at that party Binkie and you attended at the Waldorf. I looked at you and got aroused right away."

"Dan . . ." Val laughed, feeling her cheeks redden. He could always do that to her, she who had never been embarrassed by any man after the age of eighteen. Her brother Michael had encouraged her tomboy propensities, and after a while he had begun to think of her as just one of the boys. No man until Dan had been able to make her blush. He seemed to be able to do it whenever he chose. ". . . you're terrible."

"Whatever you say, angel." He chuckled into her neck as he leaned over her and loosened her pearls, then kissed each breast as the gems slid downward.

When he finished undressing Val, he began on himself, throwing his clothes any which way, stopping Val when she would have retrieved them and put them on hangers. "The hell with them. I want to get you into that water before you get a chill."

"Chill? Dan, it's very warm out tonight . . . and we are on the fringe of the desert, you know." She ambled behind him as he strode to the bathroom.

Dan spun the water spigots and filled the tub, then threw the switch for the Jacuzzi. "You can still get a chill. Desert nights are cold." He glared down at Val when she opened her mouth again. "I'm taking care of you, Val, so get used to it."

"I am used to it. Have you forgotten that we lived together for six months?"

His look brooded over her as he lowered her into the

145

warm swirling water, then followed her. "Val . . . don't," he yelped when he saw her take containers of bath salts from the shelves that lined the outside of the tub.

Val chuckled as he groaned and closed his eyes as the water frothed with sweet-smelling essence. "You're going to smell so pretty," she crooned.

"Like a damned dimestore perfume counter," Dan grumbled, sliding toward Val when she laughed. "Think you have the upper hand, do you?"

"Yes." She liked the feel of their bodies sliding together, slippery and sexy. He turned toward her, making sure that only her face and head were out of the water. "This is heavenly." Val closed her eyes, content to let Dan hold her body.

"What do you think we'll have, Val?" Dan whispered against her hair, his long legs stretched out in the huge tub.

Val's eyes snapped open. "I don't know. I've tried to picture either a boy or a girl, but I find it difficult. What would you like?"

"Either one is fine . . . but it would be nice to have a blond girl with topaz eyes like her mama."

Val sat straight up, sloshing some of the water over the sides of the recessed tub into the water alleys around the edge. "My goodness, didn't your mother tell me that you weighed ten pounds?"

"Ten pounds fourteen ounces." Dan groaned, holding her close. "You won't have such a large baby, angel. I won't let you."

"Don't be silly. You can't quarterback that, Dan Cravick."

His hands closed over her shoulders. "Val, you're too small to have such a large baby. I won't allow it."

Val felt a shudder go through his frame. "Don't start worrying, Dan. Both doctors who have examined me say that I'm fine . . . and they made no mention that a big baby would be bad for me. I don't think that way . . . and I don't

146

want you dreaming up problems that aren't there." She kissed his chin, nibbling along the strong line of his jaw.

He heaved himself and Val to a standing position with one push of those powerful arms, quickly swathing her in a fluffy towel that had been draped on the rack. Without drying himself he began to rub her body in gentle strokes with the bath towel, but not before he had slathered her body with baby oil as she directed him. "You could have caught cold."

"Not when you're putting oil on my body, silly. Oil keeps your body warm and moist." Val pushed her hands out of the towel and poured some oil on her hands to rub on Dan.

"Val . . . for crissake . . . first perfume, now body oil." Dan looked horrified at the shiny slickness of his bronzed body.

Val started to laugh at the look on his face, leaning helplessly against the wall of the bathroom, still cocooned in the bath sheets that Dan had wrapped around her.

Standing there naked, looking, to Val, like Apollo himself, he frowned at her, then the corners of his mouth lifted as though watching her laugh was all it took to make him do the same. "Damn you, wife, what are you trying to do to my image. My name will be changed to Creampuff Dan instead of Devil Dan."

Val hobbled over to him, hampered by the towels. "You look darling. I think I'll take your picture like that."

"No way." Dan rubbed his skin dry, grimaced at the shiny look to his skin, then scooped her into his arms. "Guess which lady is going to be awake all night."

"That's hardly a punishment." Val felt so happy. They hadn't played like this for such a long time. It had seemed to her, many times, as though they had forgotten the urgent reasons why she and this man had to live together, and that their need for one another had been pushed aside by the world around them that clamored for their attention—a world that left them no room for desire, love, need. She wanted to say that to him, that she felt it was time for them to get away from the world that claimed so much of them, to stop the merry-go-round that tantalized them with the brass ring but would not stop long enough for them to enjoy the beauty that they already had with each other.

When they lay on the large bed, Dan had to be reassured repeatedly that she was warm enough, then he looked at her in the light from the bedside lamp, his scrutiny minute in detail.

"Now I see the stretch marks . . . here . . . here . . ."

Val grimaced. "I don't like them." Her hand went to the side of her abdomen, scratching the white marks.

"Don't do that." Dan took her hand away and replaced it with his mouth on the same spot.

"I have . . . I have a numbing salve . . ." Val gasped, loving his face on her body, her own quivering in response.

"I'll get it." Dan left her for a moment. Val wanted to scream at him to never mind the salve. She only needed him . . . that was all she ever needed to make her mind, body, and spirit act normal, happy, fulfilled.

Dan rubbed the salve on her middle with loving absorption, smiling at Val when she tugged at his anthracite black hair. "What is it, love?"

"Stop that . . . and make love to me . . ." Val snapped.

Dan put the salve away, then began to kiss her, working from her fingertips to her shoulders, down her body to her toes and back again.

Val sighed then began a sensual search of her own. "Dan . . . Dan . . ."

"Yes . . . love . . . I'm here . . ." His voice caught as Val's hands became more feverish, more possessive. "I'll always be here."

Val was sure she exploded at his words, that she had come apart and was now floating in pieces out into the ionosphere. She felt him press her down with his body as if they could be welded together.

Their caresses became more urgent as need filled them both. Val wanted Dan to tell her more of how he would stay with her; she wanted to tell him that she loved him.

"God . . . Val . . . you make me come alive . . ." Dan's voice was hoarse.

"Dan . . . Dan I missed you so when I was in San Francisco without you."

"I couldn't sleep . . . I couldn't eat . . . the coach thought I was sick . . . and I was, Val, sick without you . . ." Dan rasped. The feelings that had always drawn them took over, dictating the caresses, the love words, as their own special rhythm of love took them away from all others.

Dan's entrance into her body, as always, was gentle, but this time there was a hesitancy that made Val impatient with him.

"Love me, Dan. Love me."

"Yes, angel, yes."

149

## CHAPTER NINE

The short while Dan and Val were in Las Vegas, they saw no one else. They wanted no one else. Sometimes Val wished that Dan would talk more about their future; if he would have told her what he thought the chance was of their marriage succeeding, she would have been happier.

She was afraid to broach the subject herself. She didn't want him to remind her of what they had both said at the onset of their relationship . . . that if either one or both felt that it was time to terminate the union, then the other would understand.

Val had no doubt she would understand why he wouldn't want to be married to her for long. There were so many pretty young things hanging around hoping and praying that Dan Cravick would notice them, but Val didn't know how she would be able to handle it when Dan left her. It was becoming harder and harder to imagine a life without him. She couldn't possibly ask him to talk more about their life together lest he did mention that verbal agreement they had made with each other.

She and Dan had made arrangements to fly back that evening to San Francisco. Now as she lay on a lounger in the semishade watching Dan sun himself, facedown next to her but in full sun, her mind tumbled with the questions she wanted answered but was afraid to ask.

"What is it, sweetie? You keep tossing and turning on your lounger. Aren't you comfortable?" Dan mumbled, still facedown on his lounger.

"Yes . . . it's comfortable . . . but I thought I would go for a swim . . ." Val swung her legs to the ground, liking the coolness of the tile under her feet, grimacing at the roundness of her tummy that had stretched her feather-light lycra swimsuit. For the first time Val decried the almost sheer look of the fabric, wishing that her burgeoning breasts were not showing so clearly from the top of her suit.

She slipped into the water at the shallow end, gasping at the coldness, then reveling at the soothing effect it was having on her skin as she breaststroked to the deeper end of the pool. She had forgotten her cap and didn't want to soak her hair in chlorinated water, so it was twisted on top, and she was relegated to doing the breaststroke, not the crawl that she preferred.

"Hi . . ." A young man surfaced next to her. "Ah . . . I don't want to sound smart . . . but would you like to make the last man on my water polo team?"

"No thanks. That's a little too rambunctious for me. You see . . ."

"Oh . . . we won't get rough or anything. I just need you to fill out the numbers. By the way, my name's Bob Weald."

"Mine's Val Cravick." Val smiled at him when he frowned and repeated her name, then shrugged. "All right, I'll make up the number, but if it gets rough, I'm getting out of the pool."

Bob's right hand came up in the air, palm outward. "I promise it won't get rough." He flung himself backward in the water toward a cluster of people treading water in the deep end. "Hey, you guys, I'm all set. Hooper, put up the baskets. Let's go."

For a few minutes Val hung back, cognizant of the baby she carried. Then the ball was thrown to her . . . and as Bob said, it didn't get rough. They didn't crowd her and they let her throw.

Val found herself screeching with the rest of her team,

151

then diving for the ball, forgetting that she didn't want her hair, tied in a topknot, to get wet.

She threw one overhand and somehow it went in. She screamed with delight.

"Atta girl, Val," Bob shouted.

She was about to fling herself forward when she was caught around the middle and lifted out of the water, even though she was in deep water.

"I thought I was the quarterback in the family, Mrs. Cravick. That was quite a throw." Dan held her above him, somehow managing to keep afloat by kicking those powerful legs.

"Thanks. It was good, wasn't it? Now you'll have to excuse me, I have to get back to my team."

Dan shook his head. "No. You'll tire yourself. I'll get you dried, then I'll take your place."

"That's not fair. The other team will have fits." Val giggled, ready to admit that she was a bit tired when Dan lifted her to the pool surround, wrapped her in a towel, and told Bob that he would be taking Val's place when the other man swam to the side to ask what was wrong.

"Hey, aren't you Dan Cravick of the Titans?" Bob flushed with pleasure.

"Yes . . . and I'm taking my wife's place . . . as soon as I get her settled in some shade." He looked at Val. "Her skin is so delicate."

Val felt all fluttery inside as she sat down to watch the rest of the game, running her hands ruefully through her wet hair.

Val couldn't take her eyes off Dan as his body arrowed into the air to catch the ball and toss it the length of the pool into the basket.

People moved to the pool area as the word went out that Devil Dan Cravick was playing water polo. The cheers of the onlookers grew, spurring on the players, but it was Dan's muscular, bronzed form that held Val's eyes.

When the game was over, Dan's team had won, but all

the players clustered round him talking to him. Dan spent a few minutes with them, talked in general to the crowd, then made his way back to Val. "Time to go, love."

They gathered their things, and Dan waved to everyone a last time before putting his arm around Val and walking with her to their suite.

He was so quiet that Val looked at him several times while she was packing their things. Dan worked right along with her but said nothing.

Even when they drove to the airport and boarded, he was silent.

"Have I done something?" Val asked him when they were seated and taxiing down the field.

Dan turned his head to look at her without lifting it from the pillow rest on the back. "I guess I was waiting for you to say something to me."

Val was puzzled. "Is this a riddle?"

Dan expelled a deep breath. "I was showing off. I wanted you to watch me . . . and not those others." He kept his eyes on her, but his firm lips tightened into a hard line. "It was dumb."

Val's brain took his words, threw them round, then sorted them. "You mean the water polo?"

"Yep. I was an ass. I just didn't want you watching those guys . . ."

"There were girls there too." Val snuggled closer to him, feeling his arm go round her, relief filling her that he wasn't angry at her. "Besides, once you began to play I didn't see anyone else. It's always like that when you play football too." She let her index finger score down his cheek. "I always watch only you."

"I was showing off for you . . . just like a high school jock," he said disgustedly into her hair. "It was stupid. I thought you'd think that."

"I love watching you and knowing that you're the best and that you're . . ." Val stopped herself before she said "mine."

"Say it, Val. Say I'm yours," he whispered, his hard arms tightening around her.

"You're mine . . . and don't you forget it." Val felt so free, as though she had unlocked invisible fetters. "Didn't I mention that once I say something I stick to it?" Val pressed her luck.

"I always thought you were a woman who knew her own mind." Dan chuckled.

On their return to San Francisco, it pleased Val to see how interested Dan was in the daily walks and workouts she took with Henderson. Immediately he joined them.

Dan also rose most mornings early enough to take Perro on a run, both the dog and the man keeping fit with jogging. Dan paid close attention when Henderson told him of Val's heartburn and how the herbal tea mix that he made her seemed to take care of it.

By the time they left San Francisco to fly back to New York to their brownstone in Manhattan, Henderson and Dan were not only friends but allies.

"You can't mean you wrote down all those recipes that Henderson told you about . . . the tea and the foods . . ." Val stared from Dan to the notebook in which he was scrawling.

"Of course." Dan looked up as the stewardess bent over him with a tray of drinks and pointed to the beer.

Val glared at the lovely redhead whose waist and tummy were flat. "I'll have seltzer water with lime, please."

Dan looked up at the tart tone in her voice, then looked at the stewardess, who was now asking the question of someone else. "Jealous? My cool Val? Never." Dan grinned when she punched him in the arm, then leaned over and whispered, "I wish I could take off all your clothes and make love to you this minute." He chuckled. "Your cheeks have little round circles of red here . . . and here . . ." His hand touched the delicate facial bones. "Wanna wrestle?"

"Yes," she snapped, then she could feel laughter filling her at their absurd conversation. "You're awful . . . the way you talk." She cuddled close to him, loving the feel of that strong, muscular body under her cheek.

New York was hot. Most days when Dan went to work out, Val took a taxi to the studio at Dan's insistence.

"If you want to work, Val, then you have to follow a few rules. Taking a taxi in this heat is one of them."

Autumn came to New York in a swirl of cool winds and soft rains, but to Val it was welcome relief from the heat.

She saw Dan even less as the real season started, and he was often on the road. Each night when they were apart they talked on the telephone.

"I thought I might buy stock in New York Telephone," Val mused one night, lying on her side on their bed as she talked to Dan and stroked Gato the cat.

"Good idea." Dan laughed. "Did you take your vitamins today?"

"Yes . . . yes . . . yes. You ask me that every night."

"It's important. How do you feel?"

"Bulbous." Val groaned, then she remembered something. "That was some pass you threw at the end of the first quarter yesterday."

"You liked that, did you?"

"Yes . . . Dan did you get hurt? I saw you holding your shoulder . . ."

"I had a feeling you might have noticed. Damn the cameraman for taking that picture. I'm all right, honey. It was just a twinge. That's the truth."

"I wish you were here." Val gulped, feeling lonely but agreeing with Dan that it wasn't good for the baby to be traveling all over. It was a relief to her to have a production job at the studio, but as she kept increasing in size, the worry that she was to have a huge baby was uppermost in her mind . . . that and missing Dan . . . missing him so much that it was a physical ache.

She had an appointment with Myrna Deitz, her obstetrician, a routine appointment. Myrna examined her, after weighing her, then both she and Val returned to the office after Val dressed.

"Val, have either you or Dan twins in the family?"

Val thought for a moment. "Not in mine . . . maybe in Dan's . . ." Her voice trailed as she stared at Myrna. "Are you saying? . . ."

Myrna nodded. "I think so. I'm getting two heartbeats. Wendy called me a short time ago and said that she suspected a multiple birth."

"Two?" Val squawked, flabbergasted, sinking back in her chair, her two hands coming up protectively over her swelling middle.

"Or more . . . but two I think," Myrna said calmly, smiling at Val. "I can see that you're not unhappy about it."

"Unhappy?" Val bleated, then she struggled to sit straighter. "Are they all right? Won't they be small? Is there any danger?"

"You are probably one of the healthiest patients I have. The walking that you're doing, the swimming, the vitamins, the vegetables, fruits, and good food you eat, all add to a basically healthy person." Myrna paused. "I always recommend that my patients keep up with their work right to the very end. It's good for them, but in your case, Val . . . well I really think you should stop working. Your body is getting cumbersome. Someone could bump you, even knock you down. I think you should consider leaving work soon, even though you have a couple of months."

Val nodded. "I'll think about it." She walked back to the studio from the doctor's office mulling over what had been said to her, the ten-block walk more bothersome to her legs than she would have imagined.

She talked to Curtis and the others and took an extended maternity leave.

She was shocked when Bud Dailey and David Curtis both told her that she would be welcome back at the

156

station whenever she chose to come. Her secretary, Jennifer, sniffed into a hankie and told her that she would personally box and deliver all Val's things to her apartment.

Val left that day with ambivalent feelings. She would miss the work and the people. They kept her from going mad while Dan was away. Still it would be nice to have the free time to furnish the nursery. She had to buy another crib!

That night on cable television she was able to watch Dan's football game. As always she was tense, her eyes glued to Dan, as though by keeping her eyes on him, she could keep the linebackers away. If they won, they would be one game away from the conference championship. That game would be played in New York, and Val would be attending.

Mrs. Hernandes brought her dinner through to the study. "I thought you would like to eat in here so that you would not miss the game."

"Thank you, Mrs. Hernandes. . . . Gato, get down, you had your dinner." Val laughed at the cat, who had followed Mrs. Hernandes into the study and was now trying to get onto Val's lap.

Mrs. Hernandes frowned at the feline and lifted him to the floor. "My sister told me that cats can be dangerous to expectant mothers, so I have had the *gato* checked very carefully." Mrs. Hernandes folded her arms over her ample bosom and nodded at Val's surprised look. "The vet said that there is no problem with this animal and that he could be near you while you are pregnant."

Gato looked at Mrs. Hernandes, then began to wash his face.

"He is smart, that one. He knows we speak of him."

When Mrs. H. brought the coffee sometime later—decaffeinated for Val because she was expecting, the older woman insisted—she brought two cups and sat and watched the game.

Gato was incensed more than once when an excitable

157

Mrs. H. tossed him off her lap as she leaped to her feet to cheer.

"He is one machismo . . . Mr. Cravick . . ." Mrs. Hernandes grinned at Val when Dan threw a touchdown pass to tie the game. The conversion sewed it up.

"He'll be coming home to play next. Would you like to see the game, Mrs. Hernandes, you and your son Juan?"

The heavy woman's face suffused with blood as she nodded. "It would be a great moment for my son to see Mr. Cravick play."

Val went to bed that night after talking to Dan, who told her that he would be getting home sometime the next day.

She couldn't sleep much that night, even propped up on pillows. Her two babies were kicking, Val thought sleepily. Isn't that just like a Cravick to keep me awake, she yawned.

She slept later the next day, and when she did wake, it took her minutes to realize that she didn't have to go into work, that David Curtis had told her that she could take a vacation until her leave started.

She rose fairly early anyway, anxious to get into the shower and cool her hot stretch marks that had gotten itchier as her pregnancy progressed.

"You look awful," she grumbled to her mirror image. "Dan will hate looking at you, you . . . you mountain you . . ."

Sighing, she stepped into the large shower stall and let the warm water sluice over her body.

After showering she slathered oils over her humpy front and as much of the rest of her as she could reach.

She had wrapped herself in a voluminous bath sheet before going back into her bedroom. She saw the overnight bag on the floor, but it didn't register until she saw Dan come through from the other bedroom where he must have showered in that connecting bath. He was still

158

rubbing his head with a towel when he saw her, his grin wide.

"Dan." Val's mouth fell open. "I thought you wouldn't be here until tonight."

"A fan flew me here in his Lear jet." Dan flung the towel to the floor and strode toward her, his arms open. "I have missed you, angel." Dan scooped her up as though she didn't look like the Goodyear dirigible and kissed her.

"Congratulations. You're the conference champions."

"On to the Super Bowl." Dan studied her mouth. "You look luscious."

"If you call looking like a beer keg luscious . . ." Val patted her middle from her vantage point in Dan's arms.

He carried her to the bed and sat down with Val in his lap. "I want to make love to you, mama-to-be. You're so sexy."

Val stared at him, seeing no mocking look in his eyes as he looked her over from ankle to ear. "What are you looking for?"

"Just checking to see that my lady is up to par." Dan kissed her nose.

She could feel his heartbeat increase under her hand and looked at him openmouthed. "How can you think I'm . . . I'm . . ."

"You're beautiful, sensual, and you drive me out of my mind," Dan stated solemnly.

Val felt pretty all at once, light, not cumbersome, svelte, not barrellike. "What was that you said about making love?"

"Can we?" Dan swallowed, watching her.

"Did you forget how?" Val simpered, plucking at the curling black hair on his chest, nibbling at his chin, all at once impatient for him. "Stop holding back . . . and run with that ball, Devil Dan." Val chuckled when she felt him ease her down on the bed and fit her close to his body. "You never used to be so reserved, football man."

The days left until Super Bowl Sunday were hectic ones. Val grew bigger. Dan grew more anxious.

The day dawned bright and clear in New York with Dan insisting that she stay home and watch it on television. Val was equally adamant that she would be at the stadium.

Dan's family and Val's were staying at the St. Regis with all in residence except the baby, Mary Val, who stayed in California with her nurse. None of them would stay at the brownstone, insisting that there was enough excitement with Dan playing and Val being in her last month of pregnancy.

That morning, when she said good-bye to Dan, she was glad that she didn't have to worry about guests. She hugged him to her. "Good luck. Be careful. Wearing the Super Bowl ring is nice, but not if you get hurt."

"I'll be fine, angel. Promise me that you won't come if you feel in the least uncomfortable. A woman having twins has to be careful." Dan spoke in measured tones.

Val saw a muscle jerk at the corner of his mouth. "I'll be fine. The family and Binkie are picking me up and taking me with them."

Dan kissed her hard, walked to the door, turned, strode back, kissed her again, and left.

It was cold in the stadium, but the sun was shining brightly and everyone was in a circus mood.

Val chattered to Dan's family, then to her own, smiling all the while.

"He'll be fine, you know," Binkie whispered to her, making Val gape at him. "Oh yes, I can see your nervousness, Valentina. Remember I've known you a long time."

"Yes, you have."

The national anthem was sung. Val watched Dan.

The coin was tossed. The Titans elected to receive.

The crowd was on its feet. Val struggled to hers, her heart in her mouth, not once taking her eyes from Dan.

Dan passed. He ran. He lateraled the ball.

It seemed to Val that he was never out of the game.

Just before the first half ended, a linebacker as big as a tank rolled through and caught Dan.

He got up, favoring his knee, looking up toward her and waving his arm.

"You see, dear," Emma Cravick said from her seat behind Val. "He's just fine."

"Yes," Val croaked.

Val watched the half-time show, laughing with the others at the comedy and symmetry of the performers. When she felt a twinge, she ignored it. She was too busy trying to imagine what Dan was doing down in the locker room.

When he ran out onto the field after the half-time show, she felt a pain in her back when she stood with the others.

The score was 7 to 0 favor of the Titans when the fullback from the other team ran through his tacklers and scored; then their kicker converted for them.

The crowd was up and down, alternately cheering and moaning as each team would fight its way down the field, then be stopped. The other team would scramble for a few yards, then it would be stopped. People were hoarse from urging their team to victory.

Val stayed seated, her eyes blinking at the rapid on-slaught of her pains. She told herself it was false labor. She was due next week or the week after.

She drank the seltzer water that Binkie poured for her.

"Val, what's wrong? Are you too hot? You're perspiring." Binkie reached up with hankie and wiped her forehead.

"What's wrong, Val?" Trevor leaned over her, his eyes narrowing on her when she gasped. "Pains?"

"Yes."

It seemed everyone in their box heard that.

Yanos roared that he would get the police. Petros tried to quiet him. Emma patted Val's shoulder.

"Should we try to get you out of here, dear?" Emma was calm.

"Ah . . . no . . . I'd like to stay where I am . . . until Dan is through, please." Val cleared her throat.

"Val, how fast are they coming?" Ruth and Carol leaned toward her.

"Beats me." Val gasped.

Binkie looked at her as though she had just announced that there was plague in the stadium. "I'll time them, Val," he whispered. "Do try to tell me accurately." He pulled a gold pencil and a leather-bound pad from his breast pocket.

"What in heaven's name are you doing?" Val asked in a normal tone, taking a deep breath and relaxing. The pain had gone for the moment.

Binkie looked at her with contempt. "I'm keeping a log, of course . . ." He reached into his vest, took out a solid gold fob watch, pressed a button that made the watch beep, then he sat back and watched her, totally ignoring the crushing action on the football field.

"Binkie . . ." Val said disgustedly. "This is not a shake-down cruise on the *Isadora*"—naming the racing sloop that Binkie sailed off Catalina Island.

"Valentina . . . don't be facetious. I do know something about birthing. Remember I was there to help my Velvet through her labor."

"I do not care to be lumped with your prize filly," Val snapped when both Carol and Ruth chortled.

"You could not be, Val. Your bloodlines aren't good enough," Binkie announced loftily.

Val turned from watching Dan on the field to give him a scathing answer when there was a twisting pain in her back. "Aaaagh." Val was surprised at the fierceness.

Yanos roared that he would get the FBI. Petros assured him that it wasn't necessary.

"Val, I'm taking you to the hospital," Trevor asserted.

"Not now." Binkie looked irritated. "I've just begun timing."

"I'm not leaving until Dan is through playing." Val

spoke at the same time, making her brother and brother-in-law frown.

"Val, you can't stay here . . . if you go into active labor. . . ." Michael pursed his lips as Binkie shushed him.

"I'm fine now. If I get uncomfortable, I'll tell you." Val did feel better. She looked from one to the other of the people in the box, each one of them watching her as though she would hatch at a moment's notice.

The third quarter ended with the teams all even still.

Dan threw a long bullet pass that was intercepted, bringing groans and roars from the crowd. People surged to their feet screaming, "Hold 'em, hold 'em!" or "Go, go, go!"

The Wisconsin team fought its way down the field. The Titans didn't give an inch without a fight, holding the other team to the ten-yard line so that they were forced to try a field goal on the fourth down. Bingo! The Wisconsin team was leading halfway into the fourth quarter.

Dan ran out onto the field, his demeanor relaxed as though he were playing a sandlot game instead of for the gold.

Val managed to mask some of the twinges that she had, but instinct told her that her twins were announcing their entry into the world.

The game advanced, and each team held the other. Val wasn't able to stand and cheer Dan, but she urged him on when she could

"Binkie . . ." Val managed, panting a little. "Try timing again, please."

"Valentina, I insist you go to the hospital." Trevor Rogers voice was determined.

"I will carry her," Yanos roared.

"No . . . no. I'll go, but Binkie will take me. The rest of you must stay here, so that if Dan looks up here, it will seem normal to him." Val pleaded, panting in earnest now as she had learned from the books she had read on natural childbirth.

"Me?" Binkie squeaked, dropping his gold watch. Only Michael's quick reflexes saved the heirloom.

"Yes, of course. Valentina is right," Emma Cravick soothed. "And of course I will go with her as well. Petros, you will see to it that Danilo is informed the moment the game is over."

"Of course." Petros leaned down to Val, patting her shoulder.

"I am going with my daughter. That is final," Trevor announced, effectively silencing all arguments.

Michael collared an attendant and whispered to him. Before many minutes there was a wheelchair for Val.

Despite her discomfort, she kept her eyes on Dan until she was out of sight of the field.

"Daddy," Val groaned as a sharper pain came. "Call Dr. Deitz and the hospital . . . and please ask the ambulance attendants if they have a radio."

Val's pains increased all during the ride so that her attention on the game wandered.

". . . Cravick has the ball, ladies and gentlemen . . . oh boy, did he get sacked . . ." The announcer seemed to relish the moment.

"Oh, Binkie . . . what did they do to him?" Val's head rolled on the cot in the ambulance, Emma and Binkie riding near her feet, the attendant taking over the timing of her pains, her father at her head.

"Not to worry, Val. Dan is tough. He can take any punishment they hand out. . . ." Binkie smiled weakly, wincing when she groaned again and rolling his eyes at Emma.

Emma glared at him. "Dan is fine, dear. He allows them to do that so that he can test them."

"Sacking is hardly a test . . ." Binkie began scathingly, then he flinched when Emma pinched him, mumbling, "I have always hated being pinched."

The hospital looked crazy to Val as she was pushed through swinging doors and down a corridor of people.

She had never realized how large people's heads were when you were lying on a gurney looking up at them. The pains were coming fast. She felt as though her whole body had been soaked in a tub, she was so wet with perspiration.

With dizzying speed she was brought into an examining room, Dr. Deitz looking down at her with a mask on her face. "Hello, Val. What's this I hear about you? That you're in such a hurry to deliver those babies."

"Yes." Val gasped, trying to smile, but all at once caught up in the whirlpool of pain.

People talked around her. Val pushed when she was told, thinking that she didn't have the breath power to sustain the pushing as the contractions lengthened.

"Here comes the first one, Val. Good girl . . . keep pushing . . . pant, pant, pant . . ." Dr. Deitz encouraged her.

"I . . . I didn't think babies came this fast. . . ." Val stammered, her breath coming in short gasps as she was ordered.

"They don't as a rule . . . you narrow-hipped gals are . . . ohhh, here's the head. . . . Number one is a boy, Val."

"Ohhhhhh . . ." Val felt perspiration drip from her forehead to her eyes as she gazed on her newborn son.

In the next hour another boy was born to Val.

"I don't feel that much better . . ." she told Dr. Deitz when she asked, craning her neck to watch the nurses with her sons. A sudden pain arched her back. "What's that?"

The doctor worked over her and murmured, "God, this one must have been hiding behind one of the others. That's why I didn't get the heartbeat. . . ."

Val stared at the little bundle. "A girl? We have a girl too . . ." Val heard the commotion and a nurse, voice raised, trying to prevent someone coming in the door. She knew it was Dan before she saw him lean over her, mask tied around his mouth, football uniform on, black smudges still under his eyes, concerned and snarling. Even

Dr. Deitz looked wide-eyed when Dan looked from Val around the room, then growled.

"Dan . . . did you win?"

"Win what?" Dan croaked, not noticing the nurse who was cloaking him in a surgical gown and mask.

"Super Bowl, silly," Val answered, sleepily.

"Oh . . . yeah . . . we won. . . . How are you? Binkie said the pains were coming fast. Mother said you were doing just as you should. Have the pains subsided? You look so tired." Dan leaned over her like a muscular tent, his eyes damp. "Does it hurt you?" He looked fierce as a tear coursed down through the grime on his face.

"Dan . . . we have two boys and a girl." Val sighed, exhausted.

"If that's what you want. We'll have one next year or the year after," he crooned, kissing her eyes, shushing her, his one hand scooping her closer to him.

"Dan, listen . . ."

"More pain?" Dan looked agonized, his eyes going round to the nurses and doctors watching him with a sort of fascinated horror. "Do something for her. Now." He barked, making two nurses jump and a doctor lean backwards.

"It's all done, Mr. Cravick." Dr. Deitz took hold of one of his treelike arms and shook him gently. "It's over. You have two sons and one daughter. Both boys weighed three pounds six ounces and the girl was an even three pounds." Dr. Deitz sounded out each syllable as though Dan had to read her lips. She tried to steady him when he staggered and looked from Val back to the doctor. "The babies are doing well on their own, but of course are in support systems."

"How's Val?" Dan croaked, watching his wife.

"Just fine . . . a little tired." Dr. Deitz patted his arm. "Would you like to sit down?"

"I want to stay with Val." Dan sounded both dazed and

166

petulant. "The babies. Where are they?" He barked, once more the deadly football field marauder.

"Right over here." Dr. Deitz gestured for Dan to follow her, but he was reluctant to release his hold on Val

"See them, Dan," Val muttered. "They're so perfect." She yawned, her hands fluttering over her strangely flattened middle.

Dan seemed to cross the floor as though it had suddenly turned into a dangerous swamp, his cleats making an alien sound as he walked. "God . . . and they're all ours. We get to keep them," he murmured, not even noticing when a nurse tittered. He turned around to Val, but she was already asleep when he whispered, "I love you, lady mine."

## CHAPTER TEN

In six weeks time Val felt like herself again, even though she often grimaced at her stretch marks, many of them on her abdomen not disappearing.

Stephen Yanos, Terrence Trevor, and Kathleen Emma Cravick were all doing well with two nurses and a doting mother seeing to their every need. Grandmother Cravick, Yanos, and Petros visited as much as they could. Surprisingly, Trevor and Binkie were almost as dutiful and devoted. Each family took the credit for having the triplets.

Val was so pleased at their health and steady growth, she didn't care who got the credit for anything.

Dan had been home much of the time since the birth of the children, and it delighted Val to see how much their father wanted to be with his dark-haired sons and his tiny daughter, almost bald but with a tiny fluff of blond hair at her crown. If he seemed to talk a tad more baby talk with little Kathleen, who could say for sure.

Life seemed to be different now to Val. There was a richness to it that she hadn't noticed before, a new clarity that held such promise. She called Henderson one day to give him a progress report on the children.

"Very well, miss, if you would really like me to come and visit the children, I shall."

"Please . . . fly out . . . and bring Perro . . ." Val insisted, all at once lonely for the man who had been such a friend to her.

"Ah . . . I don't think that I should bring the dog to the

168

house where you are keeping the children. Mr. Trevor has already invited me and the dog to stay at his home on Long Island."

"My father doesn't have a home on Long Island," Val said faintly.

"He just purchased it, miss. So I'll be staying there, miss."

"My goodness."

That night Val told Dan what Henderson had said to her. He nodded.

"My uncle Petros told me that your father was looking at property out there. . . ." He looked abstracted, gazing at her then looking at the three children sleeping in the sunniness of the lounge, the three porta-cribs taking up considerable room. "Ah . . . Val, I've told the club that I'm retiring. . . ."

"What?" Val stared at him, her mind a blank.

"Yes." He shrugged. "But since I'm still a part owner along with my mother and uncles, I said that I would take part in some team promotionals."

Still reeling with what he had told her, Val nodded.

"Tonight is a reception . . . that I said I would attend. Would you like to come with me?"

Shaken, but thinking, Val decided against it. "It's a little too soon, yet. I'll go to the next thing."

"All right." Dan's smile was stiff. "I understand."

Before Val could ask him what was bothering him, he whirled out of the room, mumbling something about taking a shower.

Since Dan was going out to dinner, Val decided to take a tray in her sitting room that was between their bedroom and the nursery.

When Nurse Atwood, who was the night nurse, assured her that the children were set for a while, Val decided to go downstairs to the lounge and visit with Dan until Bear Dulane arrived to take him to the reception

She heard the voices when she reached the foyer at the

169

foot of the stairs. Bear must have arrived early, and he and Dan were having a drink before going to the reception.

"What'd I tell ya, Dan boy. Once a woman gets babies, and three at once at that, they ain't got time for ya anymore. You'll be out cruisin' just like the rest of the good old boys." Bear had a barrel-chested laugh.

Val was immobile, wanting to go back upstairs but unable to telegraph the message to her feet.

"Not all the married men have other women, Bear." Dan sounded surly.

"Maybe not. I ain't never took a count. I'm just tellin' ya what all of 'em say about women and babies. No man counts with his wife after the babies come." There was a pause while Bear quaffed whatever he was drinking and sighed its goodness. "No matter, there are plenty of dollies around for football players. Right Dan?"

"Right. Let's get out of here."

Val didn't run back up the stairs, but she hurried so that she was on the landing and well back in the shadows of the upstairs hall when Bear and Dan left the house.

Val stood there, biting her lip, her hands clenching and unclenching at her sides. She looked at the potted philodendron that sat in the upstairs hall. She should have dropped it on Dan's head as he walked beneath her in the downstairs hall. She should have beaned the two of them before they went out the door. "Dollies, are there?" Val chewed the words and spat them out as she talked to herself. "I have your children . . . three of them, mind you, and you take yourself off and cavort with . . . *dollies.* . . ." Val fumed, feeling smoke come out of her ears.

She pretended to be asleep when Dan came home, his breath smelling of booze, his clothes in disarray. Her nostrils flared as she lay there. Was that perfume she smelled?

The next morning she brought Stephen into the bedroom to change him when he woke for his six o'clock feeding. Stephen was the most vocal of the Cravick babies. She assured Nurse Jones, the day nurse, that it was no

170

trouble to take him through to her bedroom; then he wouldn't disturb the other two.

"But, Mrs. Cravick, that's no problem. Kathleen and Terrence will waken in moments anyway." The nurse looked puzzled when Val insisted and took the bawling Stephen through to the bedroom to change him.

"Wha'? Whazzat?" Dan lifted his head from the pillow where he had been lying facedown, his cheek creased where it had been pressed into the pillow, his heavy beard shadowy black and bristly, his eyes blinking and squinting at Val.

"I'm changing Stephen, Dan. He's hungry and I didn't want him disturbing Kathleen and Terrence. I knew you wouldn't mind," she said in honey tones.

"Not mind." He ran his tongue over his dry lips, his red-rimmed eyes fixed on his squalling son. He put a hand up to his eyes and covered them for a moment.

"Tip a few last evening?" Val inquired softly, then gooed at her angry son.

"Huh? Ah . . . yah . . . some of the guys there . . . ohhh, Stephen, you do have great lungs."

"Yes, doesn't he?" his proud mother said brightly, not seeming to notice her husband's teeth-clenched groan.

"Done?" Dan inquired, opening one eye.

"Almost." His wife beamed at him. "I hope you didn't forget that my father is having a dinner-dance for the Titans. He called this morning and said that he's not holding it at the Waldorf but has decided to have it at his home." His wife cuddled their baby to her breast after telling Nurse Jones that she would feed Stephen there, in the bedroom, after the woman knocked and said that she could feed Stephen then.

Val noticed that Dan seemed to have dropped off again, so she bounced down on the bed still holding Stephen, cooing at him not to cry when she burped him. "Dan? Dan, are you listening?"

"Huh? Listening? Oh . . . sure."

171

"Good," Val continued conversationally. "So I thought I would go out and buy a new gown for the occasion, since Michael and Ruth are flying in. Isn't it too bad that Les and Carol can't make it? But, not to worry. They'll all be here for the christening. Dan? Did you hear me, Dan?" Val leaned down close to his ear and raised her voice.

"God . . . yes . . . I can hear you, Val."

That afternoon while Dan continued sleeping, Val prowled the boutiques of Manhattan, discarding all that she saw as being too conservative until she entered Chez Bijou. She had not patronized Pierre Beaumont's establishment too much because she considered the couturier a bit outré for her tastes, too avant-garde. Today she actively sought his assistance.

"Madame Cravick, I think I have just what you need, but of course, your hair can't be worn in a coronet for this creation. It will need to be worn loose, freely . . ." The artist Pierre gestured by flinging his arm in an arc. "I will call my friend Jacques while you try the dress if you wish?" One thin eyebrow raised in question.

Val exhaled. "Do that. And arrange for shoes and underthings while you're about it. This is war."

*"Belle guerre, madame. En avant marche."* Pierre's shoe-button eyes snapped with enthusiasm.

"Up the rebels," Val said weakly some moments later when the black silk creation was slipped over her head. "There's no back . . . and not much front either," she whispered to the woman who tugged and straightened the gown that clung to her form on one shoulder then slashed diagonally in the back to the spine. The other shoulder was bare, the drape of material just covering her nipples as it swagged tightly down her body until just above the knee where it flared in unpressed pleats to a very short train in the back; her legs were bare from mid-thigh down in the front whenever she moved. The fabric parted in a casual opening that disappeared when she was at rest, appearing at her slightest movement in sensual invitation.

Pierre studied her in the dress when the woman dragged Val out in front of him, his eyes sharp in clinical assessment. "Yes . . . the hair must hang over one shoulder, the covered one of course, the bare one showing nothing but skin."

"It does that all right . . ." Val muttered, looking askance at the man who minced toward her and identified himself only as Jacques. Both he and Pierre discussed her at length as though she were a mannequin and not a person.

"Your jewelry must be one earring, madame; the ear under the hair will be bare."

"I have topaz earrings . . . and a topaz slide for my hair . . ." Val offered, not even sure they heard her.

That day Dan noticed that she was cool to him. Val could see him watching her, puzzled. The charlatan! she thought.

"Your hair looks nice. Did you have it styled?" Dan said at dinner that evening.

"Yes . . . cut a little so that what wave there is shows." Val answered coolly.

"I've never seen you wear it over one shoulder like that." Dan watched her. "Very sexy."

"Thank you," Val said distantly.

"Now . . . listen . . . Val . . ." Dan looked at her, a grim expression on his face.

"Sorry. Have to check the children."

The next day Dan had a meeting with his uncles about the business. "I'll be home in plenty of time to get to the dinner at your father's."

"Good. Oh, by the way, Carol and Les are in town, and Henderson is staying out at father's . . . with Perro."

"I don't believe it," Dan said. "Is your father going through some kind of mid-life crisis?"

"I really couldn't say." Val sniffed and walked back up the stairs, flinching when she heard Dan slam the door then roar off in his car a few moments later.

173

That evening she dressed with care. Nurse Atwood came a little early, and both she and Nurse Jones watched Mrs. Hernandes help Val with her dress.

"Sweet mother of angels . . ." Mrs. Hernandes muttered, the nurses gasping behind her as Val, fully dressed, her peau de soie slippers making her figure tall, lissome, curvaceous, exciting in the black gown, the one hanging earring of topaz swinging against her cheek, her eyes glittering the same color with excitement. "Madre de Dios . . ." Mrs. H. crossed herself. "You are too beautiful. Your hair is silver-gold waves, your skin so pearly . . .

"Too much breast is showing," Val murmured.

"Yes," Mrs. Hernandes agreed. "It is a good thing you have this long cloak. Mr. Cravick would lock you up." She nodded her head, her lips pursed, but her eyes pleased.

Val was wearing the floor-length cape when Dan walked into the lounge, looking black devil exciting in his evening clothes, the silk jacket sitting on his shoulders as though his tailor had fitted it to him that moment, the silk trousers not disguising the strong, muscular body.

"Too damned sexy for his own good." Val refused a drink, watching him.

"What did you say, Val?"

"I said, time to go."

They drove out to Long Island to the accompaniment of stereo music, neither one having much to say.

Val could sense the tension in Dan, knew that he wanted her to say something to him, anything, but he was as proud as she was.

The long curving drive that led up to the house overlooking the Sound showed the lights coming from the house, cars lining the drive.

"Your father must have invited the world," Dan rasped.

"No doubt. He and Binkie decided this was a good way to announce their joint ownership in Binkie's half of the Titans."

"The family that owns together will tear each other's throats out together," Dan pointed out moodily, taking her arm as they entered the wide front doors.

Val felt a frisson of panic as she stood in the spacious center hall that bisected the front portion of the house with lounge and dining room to the left and library and study to the right, the kitchen along the back with morning room and solarium; Val remembered her father's description.

She stared at the curving stairway that hugged one rounded wall of the two-story foyer. "I need to find a ladies' room." She smiled at a uniformed maid, inclining her head. The maid smiled and pointed up the stairs.

"Let me take your cape first." Dan reached out for her.

"No." Val skipped out of reach, making his eyes narrow on her. "I'll just take it upstairs with me." She looked past Dan. "Oh, there's Father."

When Dan turned to greet his father-in-law, Val headed up the stairs, not running exactly, but moving with a determined stride. Dan's head swiveled round to watch her ascent up the stairs.

Val didn't take a breath until she was shown into the large bedroom where other women were milling.

Some Val recognized, some were strangers to her.

"Val . . ." Carol squeaked, coming up behind her sister as Val was removing her cape. "Isn't it great that we could come . . . Good grief . . . that dress . . ." Carol's mouth was agape as she studied her older sister.

"You'll catch flies, Carol," Val tittered, her eyes lighting on Ruth as the other woman walked toward them in measured steps. "Hi, Ruth."

" 'Lo." Ruth looked Val up and down and sideways. "Absolutely *the* dress of your life, Val. It's a wonder old Devil Dan let you out with it on . . . not that much of it is on you." Ruth covered her mouth and giggled, earning a frown from Val.

"Val, my dear, that dress is absolutely smashing,"

175

Emma Cravick said. "Your figure is beautiful, dear. How did you get it back to normal so fast after triplets?" Her mother-in-law kissed her cheek and smiled at her serenely. "Do take that look off your face, Val. I am not one of the hollering Cravicks. I leave that to Danilo and Yanos."

"Her figure isn't exactly the same. . . ." Carol muttered, staring at her sister. "How did you get so busty? Oh, don't glare at me. That's what half the males here tonight will be asking."

"I'm going home," Val whispered, her voice husky.

"Tch, tch, my dear. You'll do no such thing. I taught my Danilo the same sort of a lesson when I thought he was taking me for granted," Emma pronounced, making the other three stare at her. "I swam nude off the island of Keros when we took a vacation there to visit some of the Cravick family. Danilo thought it was fine to go off and leave me with his old aunts and his grandmother." She pursed her lips. "I swam when I knew he would be on the beach. He didn't leave my side after that."

"Is that what we're doing?" Ruth looked over each shoulder as though the other women in the room were enemy agents. "We're going to teach Devil Dan a lesson?" Ruth squeaked and closed her eyes for a moment. "I think it would be safer to go skin diving with a tiger shark."

"Don't be so fainthearted, Ruth," Carol snapped. "All men need a lesson now and then. Dan Cravick is no different from any other man."

"Other than the fact that he could easily throw the three of us in a long pass across the island, I would say he is much like other men," Ruth riposted to Carol.

"Ummm," Carol mulled. "I can't outrun him, but if we each go in a different direction . . ."

"Don't be silly; Danilo is civilized . . . now . . ." Emma assured them.

"That's the answer, Ruth. We'll hide behind his mother," Carol announced on a relieved sigh.

"Stop it," Val stated, giving her hair a final pat as she checked her appearance in the mirror.

"Oh, dear . . ." Ruth moaned. "You're going through with this, aren't you? Don't you care that he'll strangle all of us?"

Emma patted Val on the back. "I think you are right to do this. If I know my son . . . and I do, he has done something clumsy and explained nothing. Correct?"

"Close." Val couldn't tell them about the conversation she had overheard Dan having with Bear. She still ground her teeth at the memory. "Let's just say that chauvinism is as out of date as the Model T Ford. I would just like to remind a few men of that."

Val tried to still the quaver in her voice. Dan wouldn't kill her! She knew Dan. His bark was always worse than his bite. What would he do? She blanked her mind and tried to smile at the three women in front of her.

"You know every once in a while, Les gets a little off the track. . . ." Carol mused, reaching into her cosmetic bag and taking out her mascara and shadow to add a touch more makeup to her eyes. "They can all use a lesson now and then."

"Onward." Emma raised her fist.

Ruth closed her eyes. *"Nos moraturi te salutamus,"* she whispered.

"That's what the gladiators used to say to Caesar." Carol beamed at Emma. "Ruth's a Phi Beta, you know."

"It means 'We, who are about to die, salute you,' I think," Val offered, her voice almost inaudible.

"Lovely. Everyone should have a battle cry." Emma glowed at Val. "Come, Carol, you take my arm. Ruth, you walk with Val."

"Lucky you." Val tried to smile at her sister-in-law.

"Yes." Ruth cleared her throat, inhaled, pushed back her shoulders, and walked with Val to the door. "I think I'll precede you instead." Ruth paused for a moment, her hand on Val's arm. "If we're going to do this, let's do it

177

right." She smiled, then grinned. "Hell, it could be fun. You wait a few minutes. I want to clear the stairs. If I know our men, they won't have gotten past the small bar your father had installed just inside the lounge. If they are standing there talking, they will have a good view of the stairs. Are you game, Val? Let's enjoy this."

Val felt her trepidation fade. After all, that was why she had bought the dress. Dan would notice her tonight! Not as the hausfrau he and Bear talked about, but as another facet of the woman she was. "I'm a hausfrau, yes, but I'm a mother, wife, career woman, intelligent conversationalist, and . . . and sensualist. . . ." She had spoken out loud but to herself.

"I couldn't agree more," Ruth startled Val by answering. "Give me a minute . . . then come along."

Val gave one last look in the mirror. As she turned to do so, the skirt flared open in front revealing an expanse of leg. She barely recognized the tall, sexy woman garbed in black silk. Eyes glittering and antique-gold with excitement, their color was just a hue away from the color of the topaz earring and topaz slide that pushed her hair to one side and over her shoulder. The bare shoulder and arm gleamed opalescent, a rich contrast to the clinging silk.

She left the room, at once engulfed by the sounds of music and laughter wafting from the lower floor.

Val paused in the upper hall, glancing down over the balustrade that curved downward to the hall. No one was on the stairs. She saw her sister and mother-in-law stationed near the men at the bar, Ruth at the bottom of the stairs throwing glances upward.

Val saw Ruth expel an audible breath as she started down, then she lifted her chin, tried to remember how she had been taught to descend, tummy tucked, head up, knees moving ahead of the hips, glide. Glide she did, feeling confidence fill her as she concentrated not on the heads beginning to look up at her, but on the voice of Mlle.

178

Lily of the Villeneuve School as Mademoiselle drilled her girls on walking, moving, sitting, standing.

Val could feel her smile widen her mouth as she thought of Mademoiselle. It surprised her when Bear Dulane moved to the bottom of the stairs and looked up at her.

"When you smiled at me like that, Val, I darn near keeled right over." Bear grinned.

Startled, Val looked down at him. She heard a muted roar at the same time and watched Dan come across the foyer, Les on one arm, Michael and Binkie on the other.

"How nice to see you, Bear." Val hurried to the bottom step, reaching out and grasping Bear's arm. "Yes, of course, I would love to dance with you. We'll go through here." Val whirled toward the library door, towing a puzzled but willing Bear into the booklined room. "Interesting, isn't it?" Val had a glassy-eyed sense of doom. Dan would be right along, the whole family streaming out behind him like a wake, she was sure. "Ah . . . there we are . . ." Val pointed to a dimly lit room off the library where the sounds of music were stronger.

The glass-walled room was festooned with hanging plants and freestanding greenery that gave the solarium a greenhouse look that was both charming and relaxing. The four-piece combo of musicians was placed in the center of an arch of bird-of-paradise flowers that Val was sure her father had had flown in from Hawaii for the occasion.

She took hold of Bear's hand and looked up at him, her smile hurting the muscles in her face as a force field of electricity sparked through the room and zapped her. Dan was in the solarium! Val kept her eyes on Bear's moving mouth, trying to read his lips. The roaring in her ears would not allow her own hearing to function as it should.

It was small comfort that she didn't have to look at anyone if she didn't choose. Bear's expansive chest made a perfect screen from the outside world.

"I'm cutting in, Bear," Dan growled, making the fine hairs on Val's body straighten to attention.

"Aw . . . c'mon Dan . . . we've just started . . ." Bear looked mulish.

"Bear . . . I'm dancing with my wife. . . ." Dan grated, his teeth coming together like he was biting steel.

"Back off, Dan . . ." Bear's head swung back and forth.

"Val . . . how nice . . . our dance . . ." Binkie swept in under Bear's arm, clutched Val, and spun her away, almost tripping her as he struggled to get her away from the two sullen men eying each other.

"Dan . . . at last . . . you're going to dance with your poor sister-in-law. I've been such a wallflower. Hi, Bear. Ruth wants to dance with you," Carol babbled, throwing all her weight on Dan's right arm.

Ruth stood there goggle-eyed in front of Bear, arms at her sides.

Val watched over Binkie's shoulder as Bear gave Ruth a smile, scooped her up in his blocky arms, and began moving around the floor.

"You might warn us when you are going through your femme fatale phase, Valentina," Binkie puffed testily, his eyes going from Dan to Bear as they moved around the ballroom-sized floor in low-grade panic. "You may have given your father his first heart attack. When he saw you float down those stairs, barely dressed, he swallowed his Jack Daniel's, rocks and all. . . ."

"Stop exaggerating, Binkie," Val said abstractedly, watching Dan through the curtain of her lashes as he moved around the floor with a chattering Carol.

"Not to mention how your husband reacted." Binkie closed his eyes. "I was standing next to him, Valentina. I felt his whole body clench . . . and he . . . hissed like a steam engine." He opened them again. "I have never felt in such jeopardy." Binkie's face changed. "I say, Val, where did you find that dress. Is it Marcona's? Great style. Knocked me out," he admitted conversationally. "I never realized you had such a great figure. . . ." He looked at her tight face. "Well . . . what I mean is . . . I never thought

180

it was bad . . . but didn't know you were that . . . well built. Great body. I was about to ask Dan about your dress, but he looked so . . . primitive when he watched you come down those stairs . . . that I thought I would wait until later. Take it he didn't pick the dress out for you?"

"You take it right."

"Didn't think so. Doesn't seem to be crazy about the creation . . . but I'll tell you, Val, you do look smashing . . . great . . . like one of those high-priced . . . well, not that . . . no need to look like that . . . what I meant was . . .

"Do shut up, sweet chum," Val said halfway between amusement and irritation.

They had danced close to the window-wall as the music ended.

"Oh, Lord . . . here comes that battleship you call a husband. God, Val, do you suppose he'll break my arms? I'm not sure I like the look on his face," Binkie muttered in horrified fascination.

Val turned round to see Dan plowing her way. She broke free of Binkie, lifted a single golden talisman rose from the vase beside her, and sailed to meet her husband, veering past him when they met in the middle of the dance floor, drawing the rose across his face. "Dan . . . dear . . . having a good time, dear? . . . have to run . . ."

"Valentina," Dan roared, ruining the piano player's arpeggio as everyone in the room stared at him and stopped what they were doing.

"See you in a bit," Val caroled, gliding out of the solarium past a giggling Emma Cravick and a puzzled Yanos, who kept telling anyone who looked his way that "it was because she had triplets . . . this is hard on a woman."

Val paused long enough to kiss Uncle Yanos and wink at Uncle Petros, who winked back.

Val hesitated at the door to the lounge, aware that she was being watched, but too agitated about Dan and the Pandora's box her wounded pride had opened to take

181

much notice. She walked to her father's side, acknowledging her brother-in-law's salute as she went by him and his whispered "you're beautiful, Val" with a nod of her head. "Father . . ." she spoke, watching as her father turned to face her, not expecting the gleam of laughter in his eyes.

"You're more my daughter than I ever thought, Valentina. Paying back Dan for something, are you?" Trevor looked her over. "You are quite, quite lovely, and I'm very proud of you . . . but if Dan paddles your behind, I wouldn't blame him."

"Well, I'm drawing the fire your way, Father. He was right behind me . . ."

Trevor Rogers looked over his daughter's head. "Do you suppose he will dismantle this house?" He pondered, patting his daughter on the hand, squeezing it when he felt the tremor. "Oh Lord, that tears it . . . here comes the entire team, I think."

Val turned around to face her husband and a group of his friends who were coming toward Val from the other side of the room.

"Val, I want to speak with you . . . *now,*" Dan demanded.

"All right . . ." Val kept her eye on a grim-faced Bear Dulane. "But I think I'd like to dance first."

Bear hurried, putting one arm on Dan's. "Now, Dan . . ." Bear said in a low roar. "We don't want no fuss here . . . but it seems to us that your little lady is trying to tell you to get lost."

Val sputtered at Bear, but he didn't seem to hear her.

"Started something now," Trevor murmured. "I should move the Tang vase, I suppose."

Val glared at her father, who seemed to be enjoying himself.

"You listen to me, Bear. Nobody tells me how to act with my wife," Dan growled.

"Do I smell sulfur?" Her father chuckled at his daughter's aggravated mien.

182

"This isn't funny . . . Dan could be hurt. . . ." Val tried to say something to Bear, but her father caught hold of her and held her back, nodding at a barn-sized black man striding purposefully toward Bear, Dan, and some of the other members of the team. "Let him handle it," Trevor said, not quite smacking his lips as he edged a Sheraton side chair closer to the wall.

"You are a sadist," his daughter whispered.

"I must be," Trevor sighed, then smiled at Corbett Smith, the running back who combined breadth, height, and speed into one of the most lethal members of the NFL.

"Hello, Val." Corbett smiled at her, then turned to Bear, placing one ham-sized hand on his shoulder. "Little buddy, we are not going to fight in Mr. Rogers's house. That isn't polite." Corbett spoke softly.

Bear looked at him, frowning for a moment. "No, it isn't polite. . . . But what about Val? I think she's mad at Dan."

"Turn him loose, Corbett." Dan gnashed his teeth, his arms hanging loose but ready, his face contorted.

"Now, Dan, I'm not letting you loose in here. So you cool your jets, man, and I'm not fooling." Corbett faced Dan, who was not only his quarterback but was also his friend.

Long seconds ticked by.

Dan exhaled and nodded once, turning away toward one of the bars in the corner of the room near them and reaching for a beer.

"Have you ever fought with Dan, Corbett?" Trevor asked casually, making Val gasp in outrage.

"Not really," the handsome running back answered. "Once we were in a donnybrook together when we were rookies in pro ball. . . ." His brown eyes snapped in remembrance, a smile lifting the corners of his mouth as he shot a glance at Dan. "Remember?"

Dan stared at his friend, then at Bear, a reluctant smile

183

starting. "We pulled a few guys off Bear, then they started on us."

"A few?" Bear squawked. "There must have been thirty of 'em."

"Twenty, maybe," Corbett grudged.

"Ten," Dan stated, his eyes still on Val. "Would you like to dance, wife?"

Val nodded, but before they could move away, Bear put his hand on Val's arm.

"I just gotta say, Val, that you are the prettiest woman I ever saw in my life . . . and that dress is beautiful."

Dan's face reddened.

"I agree with you, Bear," Corbett responded, the enthusiastic words of the other players filling the room.

Dan led her out of the lounge, across the foyer, into the library, and out into the solarium. Then he turned her in his arms, looking at her for a moment before closing his arms around her. "He's right. You are the most beautiful woman in the world . . . and that dress is . . . is . . . God, if I had ever seen you in it before we left home . . . we wouldn't have."

"You are not my keeper." Val spoke in measured tones.

"No, but you are my wife . . . and no man wants his wife to . . . to be so . . . so . . ." Dan seemed to be like a steam engine with no vent. The more he talked the more he swelled with emotion.

". . . so blatant . . . so cheap, maybe . . ."

"None of those things." Dan let off steam, making dancers around them move away.

"What then?" Val raised her chin.

"Damn you, Val. Do you know how gorgeous you are? I've had the feeling all night that I was going to have to battle my way out of here to get you home."

"That's ridiculous." Val spoke in a lower tone, her eyes watching the run of blood up his face.

"No . . . it bloody well isn't ridiculous . . . and . . ." As Dan spoke he bent closer over her, so that his body

184

umbrellaed hers. ". . . if I have to break every neck in this place . . . or on this whole damned island, I will."

"You won't have to do that, silly."

"It isn't silly . . . if you're planning to leave me, Val . . . and take the children . . ." Dan's throat worked, the muscles straining.

"Me? Leave you?" Val was dumbfounded.

"You left me before . . . to go to San Francisco." Dan sounded the words like a hammer hitting wood.

"No . . . no, I didn't leave you. I . . . I just thought . . ." Val shrugged, the words she had been about to say sounding silly all at once.

"Tell me, Val, tell me." His words fired round the room, making the dancers move out of rhythm as they watched them. "I am so damn sick of feeling as if something's come between us . . ." Dan ran his capable, sure hand through his hair, the slight tremor to it holding Val's gaze.

"Shall we go home, Dan?" Val offered, not realizing she was holding her breath until he answered.

"Yes."

Val could never remember making farewells at a party in such a way. It was a whirlwind of good-byes, with her dim awareness of her smirking relatives as Dan sailed her round the room, then fastened her cape around her and propelled her out the door.

"My God, I feel as though I am a football you just threw the length of the field." Val felt like giggling when she saw the puzzlement on his face.

He shrugged. "I want to get you home and talk to you. . . ." He groaned. "I hope those children of ours don't wake up."

"Tonight we'll let nanny handle it." Val watched the smile curve his lips and some of the tension leave his body as the Ferrari sped through the night toward Manhattan.

Val felt a building urgency as Dan locked the car in the garage off the alley that ran in the back of the brownstone.

They didn't touch one another as they walked through the kitchen to the front hall.

With mute consent, they mounted the stairs to their own room, Dan locking the door behind him before he turned to look at her. "Take off the cape." He drew a sharp breath when she did. "I can't believe how you look." He muttered, his eyes going over her in a hot, restless way. "You've always been too beautiful . . . but . . . now you're . . . you're perfect." His eyes lifted from their study of her body to her face. "It scares me." His lopsided smile had a tinge of self-mockery. "I don't want to lose you."

Val's knees turned to melting wax. "I don't want to lose you either," she whispered, her body tingling with hope.

Dan looked at her dumbfounded. "How could you lose me? I've belonged to you since that moment at the party . . . when we met."

"Have you?" Her corrosive fears seemed to be dissipating. "I suppose you would call it silly if I told you, that . . . that I was sure you would find . . . would want . . . a young thing." She sounded inane, disjointed.

"You're crazy. I told you I loved you."

"When?" Val croaked, gliding across the room to him.

"God . . . that dress. I can see your lovely legs . . . right to the thigh . . ." He ground his teeth. "I'm going to kill Bear and the rest of those guys for looking at you." He frowned down at her. "I don't want anyone to see you in that dress."

"I'll throw it away . . ." Val muttered, waving her hand at him. "When did you tell me you love me?"

"Don't throw it away." Dan leaned down to touch her bare shoulder with his mouth. "Keep it for me . . . just for me." His lips ran up to her neck. Still his arms didn't hold her; just his mouth chained her to his body.

"When did . . . you . . . tell . . . me . . . that . . . you . . . love me?" Val whispered, losing control, her body reacting to Dan as though she was his puppet.

"Huh? Oh . . . that . . . well, it was after Stephen,

Terrence, and Kathleen. I told you in front of the whole obstetrical staff. . . ."

Val pushed at that wall of a chest with one hand. "You tell me something like that when *I'm sleeping*?" She shook her fist at him. "I should punch your lights out."

"Take your best shot, lady." Dan leaned down to her as though to help her. "Just don't leave me. Don't ever leave me."

Val's fist trembled as she laid it against his face. "I love you, Danilo Cravick. How could I ever want to leave you?"

Dan scooped her up so that she was eye level with him. "Val . . . Val . . . please don't kid about that. I need you, Val. I'm going to retire now . . . maybe take more of an active part in the hotel business. . . . I've even been asked to coach the Titans. You name it, Val. What do you want me to do?"

"Live with me and our children and do the job that makes you happy. I don't want you to quit playing ball . . ."

Dan's eyes glittered over her. "It's time to quit, lady mine. I might coach. I'll see, but I will take a bigger interest in the business." Dan grinned at her. "Uncle Yanos would like that."

Val felt comfortable being suspended off the floor by Dan, but she could feel her dress slipping. "Dan . . . my dress . . ."

His eyes fixed on her breasts as the dress slid lower. "So pearly . . ." His voice was thick. "Love that dress . . . God, Val, all the silly things keeping us apart . . . damn stupidity."

"Pride," Val pronounced, deciding to let Dan worry about the dress. "When I first met your uncle Yanos, he told me a story about how he lost his love . . ."

Dan nodded, his tongue touching the side of her mouth. "I know the story."

"Well, then he said something that I thought referred

187

to his life, but I see now that he was talking about us, too. Uncle Yanos is a smart man."

"Both my uncles are intelligent men," Dan agreed, then he leaned back from her. "But both of them could take lessons from that master thinker . . . your father." He grinned at her. "I got the distinct feeling that he was on my side this evening."

Val inhaled. "My father is a manipulator. He always has been." Val rubbed her face against Dan's chin, his skin already developing a stubble of beard. "Are you going to shave before we make love?"

"Don't I always?" Dan's tone was flippant, but there was a quiver in the strong arms that held her. "First, I'm going to tell you all the things I've been feeling about you . . . but did you want to say something else about Yanos?"

"Yes. After he told me his story, he finished it by saying that 'Pride squeezes love, flaws it, cuts it, and leaves it to die.' I'm sure now that he was warning us, Dan."

Dan didn't release her as he carried her over to the bed. "He said that, did he? Well, I think he's right. I think you and I have sparred long enough. It's time we forgot our worries about getting hurt . . . and faced up to what we have together."

"A great deal," Val said solemnly, leaning forward on Dan's lap as he eased the dress off the one shoulder.

"Yes . . . and we had a great deal in the beginning. I knew it, but I was afraid you didn't. It seemed to worry you that I was only two years older than you."

"It did. I saw competition for your affections in every female from six to sixty who watched you on television." Val grimaced. "I'm not proud of myself . . . and what is worse, deep down I trusted you. I knew you to be an honorable man with more integrity than any person I had ever known . . . yet my own insecurities damaged what we had."

"You weren't the only one who was childish. That first night when we met and you seemed to prefer Bear to me,

188

I was ready to take him on that night . . . and I could never rid myself of the feeling that maybe . . . just a part of you was interested in the Bear. I was ready to kill him more than once."

"If we had talked, none of this silliness would have erupted." Val, now bare from the waist up, cuddled closer to his warmth. "I overheard you and Bear talking that night you went to the reception." Val watched him frown, trying to remember. "Bear said that women lose their sex appeal after they have children . . . that's why I bought the dress." Val could feel a smile tug at her mouth as Dan threw himself back on the bed laughing, pulling her with him.

"Lady . . . I want to make love to you all the time. You were so sexy when you were pregnant, you had me pawing the ground all the time." He eased the dress the rest of the way from her body. "I was worried that our children would divert too much of your attention from me. . . ." He reddened. "I didn't like feeling like that, when I love them so much, but there it was, a feeling of jealousy of my children." Dan looked thoughtful. "That isn't there now. Now that we've talked, so much of that dark feeling is gone."

"Oh, Dan, Dan we were so stupid." Val's arms locked around his neck. "We have it all . . . and we could have thrown it away just because we didn't talk about how we feel. All that modern stuff that I subscribed to in theory went out the window when I was dealing with the man of my dreams. Fear makes false pride erupt like a volcano." Val sighed into his ear.

"Yes." Dan's arms tightened around her, his hands in tender grasp on her flesh. "You breathe into my ear one more time . . ." Dan snarled.

"Take your best shot, Devil Dan." Val laughed when he hurriedly stripped the stockings from her legs, tossing her lovely pumps to a corner of the room.

"Make love to me, Val. I need you so. Tell me again that

189

you love me . . . that we're going to be together for three hundred years." Dan held her wriggling body on top of his. "You're always brand new to me. When I think I have you mapped out, another facet of you surfaces."

In the same conversational tone, Val answered him, even as she undressed him; the habit that they had both developed of masking their feelings behind slick repartee was hard to break. "Sometimes when you were on the field . . . and someone would tackle you, I'd want to kill him. I'd shake with the need to pull that tackle apart and pummel him, yet I didn't want you to see that. I was sure you'd think it was the onslaught of dementia praecox . . . or something."

"I would have loved knowing it," Dan admitted, his hand going up her body in gentle search, making them both slur their words. "When I knew you were watching me play, the adrenaline would really pump through me. I wanted to sail through the uprights myself with the ball clutched to me, just so you'd watch me. Damn, I'm a fool about you."

"Two fools," Val whispered, her mouth at his neck.

"Yeah."

Their own special fire grew between them, heated them, coaxed them from reality into the eternal spectrum of sensual knowledge and need. They could explore this universe for a millennium and never tire of its delights. Love took them away, then settled them not so gently back on the bed.

"I like being your husband," Dan cooed.

"I like being your wife."

The soft words were a covenant that blanketed the flaw of love and buried false pride forever.

## LOOK FOR NEXT MONTH'S
## CANDLELIGHT ECSTASY ROMANCES ®

# Candlelight
## Ecstasy Romances™

**$1.95 each**

At your local bookstore or use this handy coupon for ordering:

**Dell**

**DELL BOOKS**                                            B103A
**P.O. BOX 1000, PINE BROOK, N.J. 07058-1000**

Please send me the books I have checked above. I am enclosing $ _____ (please add 75c per copy to
cover postage and handling). Send check or money order—no cash or C.O.D.'s. Please allow up to 8 weeks for
shipment.

Name _____

Address _____

City _____ State / Zip _____